P9-CDA-871

Storm
Horse

NICK GARLICK

Chicken House

SCHOLASTIC INC. / NEW YORK

First published in the United Kingdom in 2015 by Chicken House, 2 Palmer Street, Frome, Somerset BA11 1DS.

Library of Congress Cataloging-in-Publication Data available

ISBN 978-0-545-90414-8

10 9 8 7 6 5 4 3 2 1 17 18 19 20 21

Printed in the U.S.A. 23

First edition, February 2017

Book design by Carol Ly

For
Tom & Sheila Wahnsiedler
For all the years

1 * *A Storm and a Funeral*

The wind howled. Rain lashed against the windows. The ferryboat lurched as a wave of dirty brown water slammed into its side, and for one terrifying instant, Flip thought they were going to capsize. His throat closed up. The blood roared in his ears and he squeezed his eyes tight shut, expecting the sea to come crashing in around him any second.

Then the boat righted itself and plowed on through the heaving sea. It was heading for Mossum, the tiny island that was to be Flip's new home. He wasn't looking forward to it. He didn't feel happy. He'd never been to the island and he didn't know anybody who lived on it. Nobody, that is, except for the silent, forbidding figure beside him.

Uncle Andries.

Uncle Andries scared Flip. He'd scared him from the moment they'd met, two days before, when he'd arrived in the city to arrange his brother's funeral. His brother was Flip's father. And as Flip's mother had left them three years before and never been heard from since, twelve-year-old Flip was all alone in the world.

His uncle's appearance had only made him feel more alone. He'd walked into the house where Flip had been staying, looked the boy up and down, and said, "I'm your father's older brother. You will call me Uncle Andries."

He was a tall man with a big head that looked even bigger because his hair had been cut so short that the back and sides were almost bald. The sleeves of his jacket and the legs of his pants were short too and made his hands and feet stick out. He loomed over Flip like a silent giant expecting a reply.

Then he frowned. "Don't you shake hands here in the city?" he asked. "It's considered good manners where I come from."

Flip was too startled to speak. He'd never seen a picture of his uncle in his life. Even more confusing, Uncle Andries had a very thick northern accent Flip found hard to understand and he'd been busy concentrating on listening instead of offering a greeting.

"I suppose," Uncle Andries continued, "your father never bothered teaching you. That does not surprise me."

"I—I'm sorry," Flip began, finally holding out a trembling hand.

But Uncle Andries had already left the room. He took Flip back to the apartment—the apartment where Flip had lived with his father—then left to speak to the landlord. Finally he went out. When he returned, he said he'd made all the arrangements for the funeral. He also said he'd arranged with the authorities for Flip to come and live with him, and told him he should pack everything he wanted to take in two suitcases. *Only* two. Then he'd made them both supper and gone to bed. Not once had he asked Flip how he was.

He didn't ask the next day, either. The two of them got up, ate a silent breakfast, and carried their suitcases to the cemetery. There they stood at the graveside, listening to the priest intone the service. Flip did his best to pay attention, but he couldn't concentrate. He missed his dad, but he missed his mom even more. And all he could do as he stood beside his uncle was keep looking up and across the gravestones to the cemetery gates, hoping—really, really hoping—that she would come walking through them any minute. Even though she'd left them all those years ago, Flip couldn't believe his mom would leave him on his own now.

But she never appeared. And Flip's loneliness only deepened.

With a start, he realized that the service was over. He looked up to see Uncle Andries shaking the priest's hand, then scooping up some earth and letting it fall slowly onto the coffin.

"It's time to go," he said.

Less than thirty minutes later, they were in a train heading north and Flip had his face pressed to the window, watching as the canals, bridges, and bustling sidewalks of Amsterdam faded away. In their place came nothing but mile after mile of flat green fields dotted with sheep and cows. He wondered if he'd ever see his home again.

The boat heaved wildly once more, jolting Flip out of his memories. He could see a smudge of land ahead, which meant they'd nearly arrived. But the sky was even darker now and the wind even fiercer. Foam-flecked waves crashed against the side of the ferry. Flip, who'd never been anywhere near the sea in his life, was terrified. He clung grimly to his suitcases with every ghastly roll of the vessel and prayed for the journey to be over. He was certain he was going to be sick any minute. And if he wasn't sick, he thought, then it would only be because the ferry had sunk and everyone on board had drowned.

Beside him, Uncle Andries paid the weather no attention at all. He didn't even seem to know that there *was* a storm. He sat bolt upright with his arms folded across his chest and gazed out of the windows as though the sun were shining and the sea were as flat as a pond.

In the end, Flip wasn't sick. And as the minutes crept by and Mossum's harbor drew ever closer, the wind began to fade and the sea to calm. Soon the rolling stopped completely and the ferry glided gently in toward the dock. The crew threw ropes to the men on dry land to tie her fast. The other passengers gathered their belongings, ready to disembark.

But Uncle Andries remained in his seat. He stared down at Flip. "I have something to say to you," he said.

Flip, whose stomach was still rolling, waited in nervous silence.

"Your father and I were not friends," Uncle Andries said. "Did you know that?"

Flip had absolutely no idea how to reply, so all he did was nod again.

"He was lazy," Uncle Andries continued. "He didn't like working on the farm. When our father died, *your* father left and went to Amsterdam. He became a thief. This is why we never spoke after he left. Because I do not like thieves. If you want something in this world, you must earn it. You can't just take it, the way your father did."

In front of them, the passengers were lining up before the exit. Uncle Andries still hadn't moved.

"I say this," he continued, "because I want you to know what to expect from me. I did not trust my brother and I am not sure whether I trust you. I think you may have picked up many bad habits from him. But I am your new father now, so I will look after you. That is my duty. My wife, Elke, is your new mother and my daughter, Laurentia, is your new sister. You will treat them both with respect. You will also do what I say and you will not argue with me, because small boys do not argue with their fathers. And that," he finished, "is all I have to say. So now we will leave."

He got up, took his case and one of Flip's, then walked away without a backward glance. Flip followed reluctantly. In his hand was the other suitcase, the one he'd guarded jealously every inch of the way from home to the cemetery and then to the station.

That had been hard. Really hard. It was so heavy it had kept banging against his legs as he walked, no matter how much he'd shifted it from hand to hand. It was just as bad lugging it off the boat and down the gangplank because now he not only had aching fingers to deal with, but a queasy stomach and legs still wobbly from the trip across the Wadden Sea. But he never let on. He never gave a sign of how he felt. The last thing he wanted was for his uncle to discover what was in the case—it was too important to him to let that happen.

As they stepped onto dry land, the clouds above them parted and a thick, dazzling beam of sunlight shone down directly onto the dock. The vacationers ahead of them clapped their hands and let out a happy cheer.

Flip, with Uncle Andries's last words still ringing in his ears, had never felt so lonely in all his life.

2 * *Mossum*

WAITING ON A horse-drawn cart near the foot of the gangway were a blond-haired woman and a little girl. As Flip and his uncle approached, the woman climbed down and stepped forward.

"This is my wife," said Uncle Andries. "Her name is Elke. You will call her Aunt Elke."

"It's Elly," she said. "Just like everyone else on the island calls me." But she smiled as she said it and gave her husband a kiss on his cheek to welcome him home.

"I like Elke," Flip heard his uncle mutter as he put his suitcases in the cart.

"Well, you're the only one who does," she said.

But she said that with a smile too. She seemed to have a face made for smiling. It lit up the gloomy surroundings and made Flip feel just a little bit less lonely.

"I was very sorry to hear about your father," she went on. And unlike her husband, she really did look sad about her brother-in-law's death. "But now you're here, I hope you'll be happy. I hope you'll enjoy your new home."

Uncle Andries turned to the little girl waiting impatiently to be introduced. "This," he said, "is your cousin Laurentia."

"But everyone calls *me* Renske," she said, jumping down to stand beside her mother. "That's short for Laurentia. I'm seven. Our horse is called Leila. Did you really live in Amsterdam?"

Flip nodded. Both mother and daughter had the same northern accent as Uncle Andries and he had to concentrate to make out what they were saying. Growing up in Amsterdam hadn't prepared him for this, and he wondered if it would always be so difficult to understand the islanders.

"Is it true there's water everywhere you look?" Renske asked. "And do the houses keep falling into the canals? My friend Loes says the houses are always falling into the canals in Amsterdam. She's my pen pal. She writes to me. She lives in Groningen and has a television. Did you have a television?"

"No," Flip said.

"We don't either," Renske said. "We're poor."

"We're not poor!" Aunt Elly said. "We just don't have any money."

"What's the difference?" Renske asked.

"A *lot*!" Aunt Elly said.

Renske pouted. "Loes says if you don't have a television, you *must* be poor."

"I've got candles in the cupboard with more sense than your friend Loes," Aunt Elly said. "And what she knows about Amsterdam you could fit in the head of a mouse. *And* still have room left over for a bookcase."

Flip moved a little closer, to hear his aunt more clearly. He didn't realize he'd ended up standing next to the horse until both Aunt Elly and Renske stared at him.

"Well, well, well," Aunt Elly said, surprise all over her face. "She's never done *that* before."

"What?" Flip whispered nervously, wondering if he'd made a mistake.

"Leila," Renske said. "She's scared of strangers. She hardly *ever* lets anyone new get close to her."

And it was true. Leila hadn't shied away from Flip. In fact, she was leaning forward to sniff his pockets. When he turned toward her, she snorted warm air straight into his face.

"She *likes* you!" Renske giggled.

"I think she does," Aunt Elly agreed. "Do *you* like horses?" she asked Flip.

"I've never met a horse in my life," he replied. He was puzzled by Leila's behavior, but he had to admit he liked it. The horse's presence was calming. Comforting.

"Well, if they all react like that," Aunt Elly said, "you'll do fine on Mossum. We've got *lots* of horses on Mossum."

Uncle Andries was already sitting up on the front seat of the cart. "Can we get *on*?" he demanded. "I've spent quite enough time away from the farm. I've got work to catch up on."

"All you've got to catch up on is supper," Aunt Elly said, climbing up beside him. "Hendrick took care of everything and Mr. Hofstra lent a hand yesterday afternoon. Everything's doing quite nicely, thank you."

"I'll be the judge of *that*," Uncle Andries muttered.

Aunt Elly just smiled.

Flip clambered into the back of the cart next to Renske, still clutching tight to his heavy suitcase. As they moved off, he saw a girl watching him.

She was as thin as a stick, with long stringy hair so blond it was almost white. Her eyes were big and round and set in a face even paler than her hair. In her hand was a teddy bear. She didn't blink and she didn't move. She just stared. But when three young boys appeared, she darted away behind a pile of wooden pallets and vanished.

One of them threw a stone at her.

Aunt Elly sprang to her feet. "You leave that girl alone!" she shouted. "Or I'll come down there and throw something at *you*!"

The boys laughed. Aunt Elly jumped off the cart and started after them, but the moment she did so, they ran off into a big white building at the end of the street.

"Those Mesman Boys," she said to Uncle Andries, shaking her head. "They were in Mr. de Groot's garden while you were away. Got into the chicken coop and smashed all the eggs."

"Did he see them?" he asked.

"He only *heard* them," Aunt Elly said. "So of course their father said there wasn't any proof and refused to do anything about it."

"Who are the *Mesman Boys*?" Flip asked Renske.

"Their father's Mr. Mesman," she said. "He owns the hotel. Papa says he wants to own the whole island and—"

"We don't talk about the Mesmans," Uncle Andries said without looking around.

"Why not?" Renske asked.

"Because we *don't*!" he said, and that was that.

The cart rolled on into the village. It wasn't very big, not much more than two streets lined with towering elm trees that met at a crossroads in the middle. On one side of the crossroads was the hotel. On the other was a redbrick church with a tall square tower Flip had seen from the ferry. He could see big cracks at the top, under the roof. In front of the church was a sign calling for funds to help repair it.

Flip saw a butcher's and a baker's and a greengrocer's shop, a café, and a lot of small houses with white walls and gray tile roofs, tiny front gardens, and neatly trimmed hedges. It was quiet too. The only sound he could hear apart from the patter of the rain was the steady *clip clop clip* of Leila's hooves on the road.

Renske told him that there were only two cars on the island. One belonged to the doctor and the other to Mr. Mesman. Nobody else could afford one, she said, so if you wanted to go anywhere, you either walked or rode a bike or traveled in a horse-drawn cart. It wasn't anything like Amsterdam, with its rattling trams and roaring cars and people walking and talking wherever you looked. Flip had never known such stillness in all his life and he couldn't help wondering what there was to *do* on Mossum. It all seemed so boring.

Not far from the village was Uncle Andries's farm. The family lived in a small house whose ground floor was taken up almost entirely by an open, airy kitchen. It was warm and dry, without a speck of dust anywhere. Absolutely nothing like Flip's dark and shabby basement apartment in Amsterdam—the sun hadn't ever shone through the windows there.

Once inside the kitchen, Flip watched as Renske ran over to two doors in the wall and pulled them open to reveal a cupboard. When Flip looked closer, he realized that it wasn't a cupboard but a little bed, with a quilt and a rag doll on a plump pillow.

"I sleep here," she said proudly. "Papa slept here when he was a boy. And so did *his* papa."

"Isn't there a bedroom upstairs?" Flip asked.

"Yes," she said. "But only one. That's for Mama and Papa."

Then where, thought Flip, *am I going to sleep?*

He found out after supper, when Aunt Elly lit a gas lamp and led him across the farmyard and over to the barn. It was an old bent building held up by massive wooden beams. Above a couple of horse stalls and a row of concrete cow stalls and milking equipment was a wooden floor. Most of that was filled with bales of hay and straw, but in one corner was a door. Aunt Elly opened it to reveal a snug little room with a bed in one corner and a chest of drawers in the other.

"This used to be where your great-grandfather made clogs for the islanders," she said. "Back when men didn't wear anything else on their feet. We haven't used it in years, though, so we thought it would do for you. No electric light, I'm afraid—we can't afford that in here right now. But it's warm and it's dry. And it's all yours, so you won't be disturbed if you don't want to be."

She showed him how to work the lamp, then wished him good night and left. Flip unpacked his clothes and put them away. Then he slid his two suitcases under the bed. He put the heavy case at the back, so nobody could see it.

As he straightened up, he looked out of the window. Standing on the far side of the road that led to the village was the girl with the white hair. She was clutching her teddy bear and gazing up at the barn. When she saw Flip looking back, she spun around and darted away across the fields. Within less than a minute, like a ghost, she'd vanished entirely from sight.

3 * *A Thief*

FLIP *HAD* KNOWN his dad was a thief. But it had taken him a long time to realize it, even though the boxes had been around for as long as he could remember.

They'd appeared every few months or so, stacked up in the kitchen of their apartment. Flip had looked in them once and found dozens of new shirts. Another time he'd found transistor radios and watches. A third time it had been bottles of whiskey and gin and rum. When he'd asked what they were doing there, his dad had always given him the same answer.

"Oh, I'm just keeping them for a friend. He'll come and get them soon."

And until he was eight, Flip had believed him, because when he came home from school or got up the next day, the boxes would be gone. Always. He went on believing his dad until he met Willem Veen.

Willem Veen led the school's meanest gang. They loved strolling through the corridors, pushing kids to one side, knocking books out of their hands, and helping themselves to sweets or toys or anything else they liked the look of.

Anytime anybody ever resisted, or complained, or tried to fight back, Willem would always yell the same thing: "You can't hit me! My dad's a policeman! You hit me and he'll *arrest* you!"

And because everyone had seen Willem's dad in his uniform, and seen how tall and menacing he looked, they were only too ready to believe the threat. Flip certainly believed it and did his best to stay out of Willem's way. Unfortunately for him, Willem had other ideas. One day he trapped Flip in a corner of the schoolyard and jabbed a finger in his face.

"My dad knows about *your* dad," he sneered. "He says your dad's a *thief*!"

Flip hadn't the slightest idea what Willem was talking about and he said so. Willem repeated his accusation. Flip tried to ignore him and walk away, but Willem's gang had arrived by then and surrounded him. So Flip got angry.

"Well, if he *is* a thief," he demanded, "why doesn't your dad arrest him?"

"Because the police are gathering evidence," Willem said. "That's what the police do. If you weren't an idiot, you'd know that!"

"I'm not an idiot," Flip shouted, pushing him away. "But you're a *liar*!"

Willem knocked him to the ground. He knocked him to the ground when they had the same argument the following week. *And* in the weeks after that. Then one day he knocked him to the ground and stood on Flip's hands. He was wearing heavy boots that cut deep into Flip's knuckles and made them bleed.

They were still bleeding when he went home, and both his mom and his dad were there to see it. When they asked what had happened, Flip told them.

His mom rounded instantly on her husband. "Those wretched boxes!" she shouted. "Now your *son's* getting hurt because of them!"

Flip's dad didn't answer her. And he didn't look shocked. Instead he looked angry. "What did you say about them?" he demanded.

The expression on his face made Flip step back in surprise. "About what?" he asked.

"About the boxes! What did you say about the *boxes*?"

"Nothing." Flip didn't understand what was going on.

"Are you sure?"

"Positive," Flip said. "I didn't say a word."

"Good!" his dad snapped. His voice was hard and cold. "And you never will, you hear? You will never, ever say *one word* about those boxes! Do you hear me?"

Then he grabbed his jacket and stormed out of the apartment. He didn't come back until the next morning.

Flip's mother cleaned the cuts on his hands, put bandages on them, and took him out for an ice cream. They sat on a bench beside a canal and watched the ducks paddle up to beg for crumbs from the wafers. Eventually, Flip asked if what Willem Veen had said about his dad was true.

His mom sighed sadly. "Yes," she said. "It is."

"But he could go to prison," Flip said. "If he's caught."

"I know," his mom said. "And I've tried to get him to stop, but he won't. He doesn't want to." She stared down into the water. "But now you've been hurt, perhaps he'll change his mind."

"Will you ask him again?" Flip didn't want his dad to go to prison, but he didn't want to go on getting bullied at school either.

"Yes," his mom said. "I will."

"Do you promise?" Flip asked.

His mom smiled and drew a cross in the air with her finger. Then she drew a circle around the cross. Flip smiled, because that was their private sign, and whenever either of them made it, they *always* did what they'd promised. Whether it was going to bed on time, cooking something special for supper, doing homework, or going out to the movies, the cross in the circle always meant it would happen.

Flip's mom did ask. But it didn't make any difference. The boxes kept appearing. One night, Flip lay in bed listening to his parents arguing and heard his mom threaten to leave. She said she'd run away from Amsterdam and take Flip with her. His dad laughed and said she wouldn't because she didn't have any money.

"Oh yes, I do!" she shot back. "And if you're not careful, I'll use it!"

His dad was quiet after that, and for the next couple of weeks, the boxes stopped appearing. Flip felt happier. His mom even started to cheer up. It looked as though her request had worked. Then one afternoon, Flip came home to find her sitting in the kitchen, crying. He asked her what was wrong.

"He took my money," she sobbed. "All the money I'd ever saved in my life. He found it and took it. And now I've got nothing!"

"Who?" Flip asked, even though he knew what the answer would be.

"Me!" yelled his father, stomping into the kitchen. He pointed a finger at his wife. "I said you'd never leave me. And now I've made certain you won't! And don't think you can *ever* hide anything from me again. Got it?"

Two weeks later, Flip's mom left.

She went without any warning. When Flip went to school, she was at home. When he came back, she wasn't. He found his dad sitting at the kitchen table, looking at a letter.

"Your mother's gone," he said when Flip asked him what it said. "She's left us." He was so angry he could hardly get the words out of his mouth.

"Why?" Flip asked.

The only answer his dad gave was to rip the piece of paper into scraps and flush them away down the toilet. He went out without another word, leaving Flip on his own.

Which turned out to be a good thing, because it meant that when Flip found the letter under his pillow at bedtime, his dad wasn't there to tear that up too.

My dear darling Flip, it said.

I know this is a terrible thing I'm doing, and it makes me sadder than I'd ever thought I could feel. But I'm going away so I can make enough money to look after us both. I've found a job and it's going to pay me a lot. But they won't hire me if I have my son with me. And I have to stay away so I can be sure I keep everything I earn. I have to be sure it won't get stolen again. But believe me—when I've saved up what we need, I'm going to come back and get you.

I don't know when that will be, but it will be one day.

I will come back for you.

I WILL COME BACK!

Mom

At the bottom of the letter was a little cross in a little circle, and when Flip saw that, he didn't feel quite so bad anymore because he knew his mom would keep her word and return. He put the letter in the envelope and hid the envelope under the mattress.

And then he waited.

Months became a year. One year became two. The second year became the third. She sent postcards in the first few months, although Flip never managed to read them because his dad tore them up and threw them away the moment they arrived. Then they stopped for good, and all Flip had to remind him of her was the letter she'd written. When it grew dangerously worn and faded from being looked at so many times, he folded it in quarters and slid it between two thin sheets of cardboard to protect it.

By then, of course, he knew every word in it by heart and could recite it to himself in silence. But he guarded it as though it were the most valuable treasure in the world, because it was the last thing his mom had ever given him, and he had vowed never, ever to let it disappear.

As for his dad, he just went on stealing. Piles of new boxes would appear almost every week, to be collected by threatening-looking men who talked only in whispers. Sometimes the police came, but they never found anything, even though they searched the entire apartment. That was something his dad was good at: making sure they never did.

Then one day the police came, and they weren't looking for boxes.

It was Wednesday, July 6, 1966.

It was Flip's twelfth birthday.

The knock on the door woke him up at three o'clock in the morning. Two policemen were standing in the hall. They wanted to know whether Teun Bor lived there, and when Flip said yes, that was his father, they got a funny look on their faces and asked if they could come in.

One of them then produced a waterlogged wallet from his pocket, cleared his throat, and asked Flip if he recognized it. Flip did. It was his dad's. Then the policeman said that just after midnight, someone had stolen a car and driven off the road into the Brewers' Canal. Because of the dark, no one had been able to get to it in time and stop the man inside from drowning.

"But that's my dad's wallet," Flip said.

The policeman cleared his throat a second time. "I know," he said. "It was in the pocket of the man who drowned. Your father's dead, son."

4 * The Ghost Girl

Flip was plunged straight into farm life the very first morning after his arrival.

His uncle and aunt owned six fields. On five of them they kept chickens, a small herd of dairy cattle, and a large flock of sheep. The eggs the chickens laid were sold in the village shop. The milk the cows produced and the wool the sheep grew went to businesses over on the mainland.

Every morning at dawn, Uncle Andries brought the cows into the barn for milking. When he led them back to their field, he told Flip that it would be his job to clean the stalls they'd stood in and take the manure out to a pile behind the barn. When he'd finished that, his next task was to help Renske collect the eggs the chickens had laid, clean them, and stack them in cardboard boxes. After that, it was weeding time.

The sixth field was a vegetable garden. It lay at the back of the house and was packed with rows of potatoes and runner beans, onions and cabbages, and tomatoes growing on sticks against the wall in a little greenhouse beside the back door. In between the vegetables, Aunt Elly had planted bright clumps of dahlias and African violets and snapdragons to help ward off insects.

But flowers didn't stop weeds. *They* had to be removed by hand. And because the garden was so big, and because weeds grew with abandon in the warm summer heat, it was a job that kept Flip and his aunt and Renske busy until late each afternoon.

It didn't take Flip long to learn that shoveling manure, collecting and cleaning eggs, and then digging and scraping with a long-handled wooden hoe was hard work. He'd never done anything like it before in his life, and when he stopped at the end of the first day, he was so exhausted he barely had the strength to eat supper. As soon as he finished, he stumbled over to the barn and up the stairs to his room and fell asleep the moment he stretched out in bed.

It was the same the next day. And the days after that. But Flip persevered, and by the beginning of the second week, he'd begun to get the hang of things.

He learned that the trick to shoveling manure without getting it all over his shoes and pants was to collect just a small lump on the fork—not a huge one that fell apart the second he lifted it up. The best way to collect eggs without the chickens pecking his fingers to bits was to cup their heads and necks lightly with one hand, then reach under them for the eggs with the other. And when it came to the vegetable plot, he realized he had to slide the blade of the hoe right down *under* the root of the weed. That way, with a single flick the whole thing came out and not just the top. He also discovered that he had to break up the earth around each plant so it didn't flatten out and form a hard crust that pushed away water. Broken earth sucked up every drop that fell on it.

As tired as it made him, he did all this without complaining because he was convinced he wouldn't be doing it for long. He was certain that one day—one day soon—a letter would arrive to tell him that his mother had been found and would be coming to get him. He knew the police were looking for her. They'd told him so after his dad died and before Uncle Andries had arrived in Amsterdam. Yet every afternoon, when Aunt Elly walked into the village to collect the mail—the village was so small, there wasn't any need for a postman—she never returned with a letter containing any news for Flip.

One day she saw him watching and asked him what he was waiting for. He was too embarrassed to answer.

He thought she'd think he was rude and ungrateful. She insisted, though, so he told her. Much to his astonishment, she took him into the kitchen, sat him down, poured him a glass of fresh buttermilk, cut him a huge slice of apple pie, and said, "Of *course* you want to leave. You want to be with your mom. If I was in your shoes, I would too."

Flip didn't know what to say. "You're not angry?" he managed at last.

If he'd said the same thing to his dad, that he wanted to leave, then his dad *would* have been furious. And called him ungrateful. And sent him to bed.

Aunt Elly just smiled and put a scoop of fresh cream on the apple pie. "I'm impressed," she said.

"Impressed?"

"I most certainly am," she said. "Your father dies. You don't know where your mom is. You come to a strange island to live with people you've never met before *and* you have to get up early and go to work on a farm. Yet you don't complain. You don't refuse to help. I can think of children on this island who don't work half as hard as you and they've lived here all their lives. I'm *very* impressed."

"But what if I go?" Flip asked.

"It won't change the fact that you've done yourself proud while you've been here."

It had been ages since anybody had paid Flip a compliment. Years, in fact. It made him like Aunt Elly even more than he had the day he'd met her. And that night, for the first time since he'd arrived on the island, he realized there was something else he liked about it: living in the barn.

He liked the rich sweet smell of the hay and the straw, and the lingering odor of the cattle. He liked his room's dry warmth and silence. Back in Amsterdam, the walls of the apartment had all sported damp patches and it had never, ever been quiet—the sound of footsteps on the pavement outside and the rumble of passing trams had seen to that. And on Mossum he didn't have to worry about strange men knocking on the door to collect boxes at all hours. In the barn, he realized, he felt safe.

Even if he was never entirely alone.

Whenever he looked out of his window in the evenings, the girl with the pale hair would be standing on the far side of the road. She'd be standing still, with her teddy bear clutched in her hand, staring at the barn. The moment she saw Flip looking at *her*, though, she'd spin around and run away. She'd always run away.

So one day he asked Aunt Elly who she was.

"Nobody knows," she said.

"Doesn't she live on Mossum?" he asked.

His aunt shook her head. "Not all the time. She just came here for the summer, with her mother. They're living out in a cottage in the dunes. They've been here for two months now."

"What are they doing?"

"A long vacation, I think," Aunt Elly said. "The mother comes into the village to do her shopping, but she doesn't talk much to anyone. I know her name's Mrs. Elberg, but that's *all* I know. As far as I can tell, the only people she talks to are the shopkeepers, and then it's only to say what she wants to buy. Which is more than you can say for her daughter. *She* never talks at all."

"Never?" Flip asked.

Aunt Elly shook her head. "Not one word. People *see* her everywhere. In the fields. On the beach. Down at the harbor. But the moment you say anything to her, or look at her, she just runs away. Ever since she got here, that's all she's done. Run away."

"She's like a ghost," Flip said, remembering the way she'd vanished on his very first night. "She's a ghost girl."

Aunt Elly smiled sadly. "Well, that's a good name for her, poor thing. That's just what she is: a ghost. I can't imagine what happened to make her like that."

And from that moment on, that's what she became to Flip: the Ghost Girl.

He had absolutely no idea that the very next day, she was going to change his life forever.

5 * Confusion

It was Saturday, and once Flip had cleaned the cow stalls and collected the eggs, Aunt Elly called him into the kitchen and handed him a ten-cent coin. Renske got five cents. When Renske asked why Flip got more pocket money than her, her mother said it was because he was older, *and* it was the end of his second week on the island.

"You've done nothing but work since you arrived," she said, turning to face him. "I let you do it because I thought it would help take your mind off what happened to your father. But now it's time you had a break. It's time you saw a little more of Mossum. There's a lot more to it than tidying manure piles and weeding. So the rest of the day is for *you*."

And the next thing Flip knew, Aunt Elly was guiding him out through the door and telling him all he had to do was be back by lunchtime. As he stood on the porch, wondering where to go, he heard Renske explaining that Flip had lived on the farm for two weeks and she'd lived there for seven years, so if anybody should get more pocket money, it should be *her.*

Flip wandered along toward the village. He'd seen it just the once, when he arrived, and then only briefly, so this time he paid more attention. Renske had already told him about the number of cars, so their absence wasn't a surprise, but what did surprise him was the television antennas. There weren't any. On *any* of the houses.

Then there were the shops. Mossum didn't have a supermarket. All it had were strange little shops with everything for sale stacked up on shelves behind a high wood or glass counter, so that you had to ask for what you wanted. They even had old-fashioned weighing scales he'd only ever seen before in books.

The islanders were stranger still. The men all had really short hair and wore thick wooden clogs. The women all wore pinafores to protect their dresses. There wasn't a pair of jeans in sight. Or a leather jacket or a pair of sneakers like some of the kids in his school had had. He almost felt like he was walking around in a museum.

At the entrance to one of the shops, he bumped into a man who looked down at him and said something Flip didn't understand at all. So he just nodded politely and went inside to buy some Bazooka Joe bubble gum. The shopkeeper and his three customers fell silent as he entered. Then the shopkeeper spoke and this time Flip recognized the word *Amsterdam*. But *nothing else*!

The grown-ups laughed.

Was he stupid? Flip asked himself. What was wrong with him? Why didn't he understand them?

The shopkeeper came around the counter and gave him a friendly pat on the shoulder. "Don't worry," he said, smiling. "I was just saying it was the boy from Amsterdam and asking you what it was like living on our little island. Quite a change for you, I shouldn't wonder. Now, what would you like?"

Flip asked for some bubble gum and was given two for the price of one. "For being a good sport," the shopkeeper said.

Flip didn't know what that meant, either, and only found out when he bumped into Mr. Bouten on a path leading off to some woods beyond the village.

Mr. Bouten helped Uncle Andries on the farm three days a week. He was an old man with a big flat nose that looked like somebody had jumped on it, and a crooked leg that made him lurch from side to side when he walked. He wore faded blue overalls, a black beret, and massive wooden clogs that scraped on the ground with each step.

"You will call him Mr. Bouten," Uncle Andries had said the first time they'd met. As soon as he'd walked away, though, the old man had winked to Flip and whispered, "But you can call me Hendrick when he's not around."

Flip never had called him that—he couldn't get used to calling grown-ups by their first names—but even so, he liked Mr. Bouten, who always seemed happy to see him. That morning was no exception.

"Hello, Flip," he said with a smile. "Got a day off, have you?"

Flip nodded. "Aunt Elly said I should explore the island."

"Well, you've got a good morning for it," Mr. Bouten said. "But I wouldn't stay out too long if I were you. Storm's coming."

Flip looked up at the sky. The sun was shining; there was hardly any wind and only a few thin white clouds on the horizon. It was lovely weather.

"Oh yes," Mr. Bouten said, noticing his puzzled look. "It's going to rain, all right. Take my word for it. But tell me," he added, "what have you seen so far?"

"A bit of the village," Flip said. And then because he was pretty certain Mr. Bouten wouldn't laugh at him, he explained about not understanding what anyone had said.

"Ah," said Mr. Bouten. "Well, up here we speak two languages: our own one, Fries, and the Dutch you all speak in the rest of the country. We have to know that, otherwise we couldn't talk to the vacationers." He smiled again. "So the next time someone says something and you don't understand, you answer in Dutch. They'll understand you, I guarantee it." Abruptly, he turned and pointed at the woods behind him. "But you don't want to waste your time talking to me. If you're out *exploring*, you should try in there."

"Why?" Flip asked.

Mr. Bouten smiled. "Well, it wouldn't be exploring if you knew what it was, now, would it?" And without another word, away he limped toward the village.

Curious, Flip set off in the opposite direction.

6 * *Bomber*

Stepping into the woods was like stepping through a door into a new world. Within just five paces, Flip was surrounded by towering pine trees, walking on a thick carpet of dead pine needles. If the island was quiet, here it was more so. The trees shut out the breeze. The needles muffled his footsteps. He was engulfed in silence and shadows.

He walked on until his way forward was blocked by a massive tangle of weeds and brambles. Just as he was about to turn back, he spotted a path that led *into* the tangle. He followed it, only to see it narrow to a tunnel that forced him to get down and crawl on his hands and knees. When he emerged at the far end, he was in a ragged clearing open to the sky. And there, directly in front of him, was the most amazing sight he'd ever laid eyes on.

It was the wreck of a World War Two bomber. Its nose was buried deep in the earth, while the tail had come to rest on a jumble of broken tree trunks and stuck up like an arm pointing at the sky. The left wing had been ripped away, leaving a gash down one side big enough to climb through.

There wasn't anyone else in sight, so, treading carefully, Flip pulled himself up inside the plane and crept through the fuselage to the cockpit. The leather on the pilots' seats had long since rotted away, leaving only the springs and metal frames. The joysticks had vanished. Every dial in the instrument panel had been ripped out. But there was no missing the line of jagged bullet holes beside the pilot's seat, and a foot-size gash in the floor in front of the copilot.

"Can you see the bloodstains?"

The voice was so unexpected, Flip jumped. When he got his breath back and peered outside, he saw the three Mesman Boys, standing in a semicircle.

He'd seen them a few times since his arrival on Mossum, walking past the farm, carrying strings of dead birds they'd shot with their slingshots. Renske had told him their names, so he knew who they all were. Jan was the oldest. He was thirteen. Petrus and Thijs were twins. They were eleven. All three wore leather boots that came up to their ankles, gray shorts, and white short-sleeved shirts with the top button closed. They had the same short haircuts as Uncle Andries, which made their ears stick out from the sides of their heads like pegs. That morning, as ever, three dead crows hung from the boys' belts by their tail feathers.

"We saw you coming and hid," Jan said, laughing. "Thought it would be funny to scare you." Then he pointed with his slingshot. "Look at the instrument panel. And that big hole in the floor. Isn't it great? I bet the pilots got blown to *pieces* before they crashed!" he added with a grin.

Sun and wind and rain had long since faded the stains, but now that he knew where they were, Flip could just make them out. He didn't think it was great, though. Back in Amsterdam, he'd had a friend whose uncle had flown a fighter for the RAF in the war and been shot down. Flip had seen him once, limping along the street with the left sleeve of his jacket flapping empty because he'd lost his arm when he'd crashed. He hadn't looked as though it had been great getting shot to pieces.

"It's a British bomber," Jan said. "Crashed here in 1944. After bombing Germany."

"And it's *haunted*," Thijs added.

"People in the village say you can hear the dead Englishmen moaning at night," Petrus said.

Jan shook his head at his younger brothers, but the look in their eyes said the twins believed every word.

"Actually," Flip said, "it's American."

Jan frowned. "What do you mean, American?"

"It's a Martin B-26 Marauder," Flip said. "It's an American plane. It had a crew of seven and machine guns in the front, the middle, and the back. It had drop tanks so it could fly all the way to Germany on bombing missions, and it could carry up to two tons of bombs."

In an instant, Flip knew he'd said something wrong. All three boys' eyes narrowed and they stood up straight and folded their arms across their chests.

"How do *you* know?" Jan asked.

"I read it in a book," Flip said. Which he had, back in the school library a year before. The library had been the one place he'd been safe from Willem Veen and he'd spent as much of his free time in it as he could.

"Oh, really?" Jan said. "Show me."

"What?" Flip said.

"This *book* of yours," Jan said. "Because *our* dad told us it was British. So I want to see this book that makes you say he's a liar."

"I didn't say he was a liar," Flip said.

"Yes, you did," Petrus said. "*He* told us it was British. *You* say it's American."

"So you're calling him a liar," Thijs concluded.

Flip was so startled by what was happening—and how *fast* it was happening—that he didn't know what to say. Or what to do. In the silence, Jan leaned forward and rested his hands against the fuselage.

"You too rude to answer?" he demanded. "Don't they teach you any manners in Amsterdam?"

"Our father says they're all like that in Amsterdam," Petrus said. "They think they know best. About everything."

Not to be outdone by his brothers, Thijs joined in. "And look how long his hair is. Like a girl's."

Flip didn't think his hair was long. It just covered the tops of his ears, and he'd seen pop groups in magazines with hair much longer than that.

"Perhaps you *are* a girl," Thijs said.

"I'm not a girl!" Flip said.

"Then prove it," Jan said.

"How?"

"Fight me."

The three brothers instantly spread out again in a semicircle. Flip, his heart pounding in his chest, recognized the maneuver. It was the way Willem Veen and his friends had always arranged themselves before a fight so that if Willem began to lose, the boys on either side of him could jump in and help. Flip knew he didn't stand a chance of winning against the three of them.

Jan took a step forward. But the moment he did so, a siren began to wail in the distance. All three brothers looked at each other.

"*Lifeboat!*" they yelled in unison, faces lit up with excitement.

Jan turned and ran for the tunnel. His brothers sprinted after him. Within seconds, they'd vanished.

Flip stayed where he was as the siren continued to wail. A minute later, unable to contain his curiosity, he jumped down out of the cockpit and ran after them.

7 * Storm Horses

IT HAD BEEN sunny when Flip had entered the woods. But now, when he emerged from the tunnel, it was to see the sky a forbidding dark gray, with clouds stretched across the island from horizon to horizon. The tops of the trees behind him were creaking and waving in the wind.

The Mesman Boys were far away, heads down, running as fast as they could. He ran after them until he came to Uncle Andries's farm, where he saw his uncle leading Leila out of her field and heading off at a run away from the village. Behind him came Mr. Bouten, wheeling his bike.

"What's happening?" Flip asked.

"The siren's calling the lifeboat out," Mr. Bouten said.

Flip pointed at Leila. "Why do you need a horse for a lifeboat?" he asked.

"Jump on," Mr. Bouten said, "and I'll show you."

So Flip perched on the bag rack behind the seat and off they went. Soon they reached a wide brick building set in low-lying sand dunes. It had a wooden roof and giant doors that took up the whole front wall. Gathered before it was a group of men and eight other horses: all big, sturdy farm animals. As Flip jumped down from the bike, three men rolled the doors back to reveal a blue-hulled lifeboat.

It was sitting in a white metal cradle mounted on two massive iron caterpillar tracks. The moment the doors opened, the men ran inside and emerged with coils of rope and thick canvas harnesses and bridles. Within minutes, eight of the nine horses—all but Leila—had been lined up in pairs in front of the lifeboat and harnessed to metal hooks on the front of the trailer.

While this was happening, Mr. Bouten went inside and unfastened a rope attached to a metal cleat on the wall. Down from the ceiling dropped eight pairs of green rubber wading boots, the kind that came up to a man's chest. He loaded them into a horse-drawn cart behind the lifeboat, then piled on waterproof jackets, pants, and hats, more ropes, and a thick wooden pole.

At the front of the cart, Uncle Andries was harnessing Leila between its shafts. Mr. Bouten grabbed the reins and climbed up onto the seat. He beckoned Flip to join him and pulled a whistle from his pocket with the other hand. With one long shrill blast, he signaled the men who'd brought the horses to the lifeboat house to urge them forward.

The horses bent their heads, dug their hooves into the sand, and heaved. Every muscle in their necks stood out with the strain. Metal horseshoes slipped and skidded on the bricks before the door. Then the lifeboat lurched, rolled forward, and kept rolling, picking up speed with every yard. The men trotted along beside their horses. A couple of them had long waving whips and gave them a crack from time to time to urge the horses on. And at the back, head up and keeping pace with the others easily, came Leila. The wheels of the cart left the sandy path and thrummed along the surface of the road.

Flip glanced behind him and saw the Mesman Boys standing by the empty lifeboat house, watching him enviously as he rode away out of sight.

The rain drummed down. The caterpillar treads rumbled and clanked as the men's heavy boots and clogs pounded along the road, keeping time with the clatter of the horses' hooves. Manes and tails shook. Harnesses jingled. The lifeboat rolled past Uncle Andries's farm, skirted the village, and took a path that led off to the northern shore of the island. When it reached a gap in the dunes it kept going, down a long slope and out onto the open sand.

In his two weeks on Mossum, Flip had never been down to the beach, and the sudden vast expanse of sand and sky took his breath away. It stretched off in all directions for as far as he could see and made him feel about as big as a matchstick on a soccer field.

But there was no time to sit and stare. The moment the horses stopped at the water's edge, the lifeboat men sprang into action. Two of them grabbed a heavy anchor fixed to the back of the lifeboat trailer by a chain and hammered it into the sand. Uncle Andries and four other men started getting dressed in the yellow waterproof clothes. Mr. Bouten pulled on a pair of green waders, grabbed the pole from the back of the cart, and strode out into the surf in front of the lifeboat.

He paced back and forth, ignoring the waves crashing against him. All his concentration was focused on finding a good flat spot for the lifeboat trailer. When he found it, he jabbed the pole into the sand and raised his hand.

On the beach, the horses had all been unfastened and split into two groups of four. One group was led to the right, the other to the left. Mr. Bouten strode back up the beach to stand beside Flip and they watched as the ropes attached to the canvas harnesses were clipped to heavy iron rings at the rear of the lifeboat trailer.

Flip looked into the thick rolling waves crashing onto the beach and shuddered. He'd never learned to swim and the sight of such a vast stormy sea made him nervous. He couldn't imagine what it did to the horses.

"Aren't they scared?" he asked Mr. Bouten.

"A little perhaps," the old man replied. "Like we all are, your uncle included. But they're brave. And this is a job they do. A brave horse likes doing a good job. And they know we're here with them and won't leave them. That makes a big difference. They know they can trust us. Trust's important to a horse."

With everything now ready, Mr. Bouten stepped forward and let out a second blast on his whistle. Once more the horses bent to their task and heaved the life-boat trailer forward. They didn't hesitate. They strode straight out into the sea and kept going until the men guiding them brought them to a halt. The water crashed around their flanks, but they stood patiently in the surf, attentive to the calming words at their backs.

Flip marveled at that calm, at the way the animals responded to just the tiniest encouraging nudge or word from their owners. He no longer felt nervous. Watching these eight horses brave the power of the incoming waves sent a thrill like electricity prickling through his whole body. It was as if a door had been opened into a part of him he'd never known existed and he felt so suddenly alive he wanted to laugh and shout out loud.

And then, so quickly he almost missed it, the lifeboat was sliding free and into the waves with the men on board gathered at the stern, huddled behind the wheelhouse. The engine turned over. The propellers churned. Out to sea it went, spray crashing up over the bow. Soon it had been swallowed up in the rain and was no more than a blur heading for the horizon.

The men left on the beach sighed with relief and started unhooking the horses and leading them back up onto dry land.

"Now you see why we need horses for a lifeboat," Mr. Bouten said to Flip. He was shaving a splinter of broken wood off the side of the cart with a big pocketknife. "Best way to get the boat into the sea. Especially when there isn't enough money for one of them new motorized trailers."

"What happens now?"

"Now," Mr. Bouten said, "we get the trailer ready for when the lifeboat returns. When it does, the horses will pull it up out of the water. And then it's back to the lifeboat house."

"Where *is* the lifeboat going?"

"There's a boat taking horses to Ameland," Mr. Bouten said. "Run into trouble near Hook Start. Don't know any more than that. Heard nothing since the first distress call." He folded the knife shut and slipped it back into his jacket pocket.

"Can I stay and watch?" Flip asked. He didn't want to leave the horses. Or this broad beach out under the dark, looming sky. It was all like nothing he'd ever known and he didn't want it to end.

Mr. Bouten shook his head. "You're going straight back home," he said. "I don't want your aunt worrying where you are. Or getting angry with me for keeping you out in the rain. I'd rather face a Force Ten gale than your aunt when she's angry. Can you find your way back by yourself?"

Flip said he could and reluctantly, very reluctantly, set off up the beach and into the dunes. He hadn't gone more than a few steps into them when he heard a familiar voice.

"What makes *you* so special, city boy?"

It was Jan Mesman. He was standing halfway up a dune in front of him, beside his brother Thijs. They had their slingshots in their hands.

"How come *you* get to ride on the cart?" demanded a voice at his rear. It was Petrus, blocking any retreat.

He had his slingshot out too, and was fitting a stone into the sling. "We've lived here longer than you, and that Bouten bloke never let *us* ride on the cart."

"It's *Mr.* Bouten!" Flip said.

"He's just a farmer," Jan said. "Nobody calls *farmers* Mister. And *you* don't tell *me* what to call anyone. I'll call anyone what I like." He loaded his slingshot and took aim at Flip. "Maybe this'll make you learn."

A split second before Jan fired, Flip ducked. The stone buzzed straight past his head and smacked into Petrus's knee. Petrus let out a wail of pain and collapsed in a heap. As Jan and Thijs stood staring in disbelief, Flip seized his chance and ran.

8 * The Ghost

FLIP HADN'T GONE more than a few feet down the path when he heard a snap. A second later, there was another snap. And then a third. As he ran he glanced behind him and saw all three brothers fire at once.

One stone hit the ground in front of him. The second buzzed angrily past his head. The third struck him right in the middle of his back.

The pain was hot and scalding. It felt as though somebody had taken a massive nail with an extra-sharp point and hammered it between his shoulder blades. Flip staggered and fell to one knee.

But doing that saved him because, as he dropped, the brothers loosed another volley that shot past uselessly overhead. While they stopped to dig fresh ammunition out of their pockets, Flip cut right and ran for the trees dead ahead. He wasn't sure where he was, but that didn't matter. If he could just hide and wait until the brothers got bored looking for him, then he'd slip off home.

Then he *did* recognize his surroundings. He was heading for the woods that held the wrecked bomber. There was the path between the trees and the tunnel that led into the clearing. He hurled himself down it and stopped, heart pounding and breath rasping, when he reached the remains of the plane.

A few seconds later, he realized that he'd made a mistake.

Because there was no other way out. Wherever he looked, thick clumps of brambles blocked any exit other than the path he'd just taken. And that, he realized as he heard feet thumping on the earth, was the one the Mesman Boys were coming down.

The brothers stormed into the clearing and stopped. When they saw Flip standing with his back to the bomber and nowhere to go, they smiled. Then they fanned out, loaded up all three slingshots, and took aim.

It hadn't been slingshots back in Amsterdam, but it had been Willem Veen and his gang against Flip, and Flip had always lost. He'd never had a chance. But he had a chance now, so he grabbed it. He charged straight at Jan, who was too startled to fire his slingshot, and grabbed him around the waist.

It almost worked. With Flip holding so tight to him, Thijs and Petrus didn't dare fire in case they hit their brother. They just stood there not knowing what to do. But before Flip could manhandle Jan over to the exit and escape again, Jan wriggled free and knocked *him* down.

This time, there was nothing he could do to stop them. Thijs and Petrus ran in and held Flip's legs down while Jan knelt on his arms and started punching. He punched him in the stomach and the arms and the shoulders, then hit him twice in the side of his head.

He was lifting his fist for a blow to Flip's nose when something went *BOOM!*

The Mesman Boys froze, staring at each other in shock. Before either of them could speak, there was another *BOOM*, much louder this time and more drawn out. It seemed to be coming from the bomber.

"It's a joke," Jan said. "Someone's playing a joke."

He laughed. But Thijs and Petrus didn't. Their faces went pale and they jumped up and stared frantically all around them.

"It's the ghost," Petrus said.

"There's no ghost," Jan said. "Don't be so stupid!"

But the moment the words were out of his mouth, there came another *BOOM*, louder and heavier than before, followed by a fourth, louder still.

And then the clearing seemed to explode as *BOOM* followed *BOOM* in an ever-increasing crescendo that made the plane roar and vibrate, as though a giant were smashing a hammer against the inside of the biggest metal trash can in the world.

It was too much for Petrus and Thijs. Faces white and eyes wide with fear, they spun around and shot into the tunnel as though they'd been fired from a gun.

Jan tried standing his ground, but without his brothers he wasn't so brave. Five seconds after they disappeared, he took right off after them.

As abruptly as it had begun, the banging stopped. Soon all there was to hear was the distant sigh of the wind in the trees. Flip didn't believe in ghosts—he never had—but even so, all alone in the clearing beside the deserted plane, he felt small and very vulnerable.

"Is someone there?" he called out.

Silence.

"They're gone," he added.

Up above him, he heard a sound. When he looked up, he saw a face peering down at him from the rear gunner's turret.

It was the Ghost Girl.

She didn't smile. She didn't say anything. She just looked at him.

"Did *you* make that noise?" Flip asked.

She nodded. Once.

"How?"

She lifted her left hand and showed him a large flat square of wood, the kind bricklayers used to hold wet cement.

"Did you do it to frighten them away?"

She nodded.

"Why?"

She held up her right hand, showing him the battered teddy bear clutched in her fingers. Flip could see now that it had a missing arm, a missing leg, and a missing eye.

"Did the Mesman Boys do that?"

She nodded again and went on staring down at him.

"Do you ever talk?" Flip asked.

She shook her head.

"*Can* you talk?"

A nod.

"But you don't want to?"

Another nod. Then something behind her made her pull her head back inside the turret.

When she didn't reappear, Flip peered up through the fuselage into the tail. There were metal struts on the inside, so he used them to climb up to her. She was standing on the edge of the rear gunner's seat, peering out over the tops of the trees toward the sea. The sky was still dark and the wind was still roaring in over the waves crashing onto the beach. A fresh gust of rain spattered down on their upturned faces.

"We should go," Flip said.

The Ghost Girl ignored him. She leaned as far as she could out of the turret, staring intently into the distance.

"We'll get wet."

She shook her head again, furiously this time, and jabbed her finger toward the beach. Flip looked, but didn't see anything.

"Well, I'm going to go," he said, and started to climb down.

The Ghost Girl grabbed his hand, pushed him against the side of the plane, and pointed. Her eyes were wide with fright.

He spotted a movement in the sea. Something dark. It vanished as a wave swept over it and then reappeared a second or two later. He still couldn't make it out clearly, but he could see it moving up and down and from side to side, as if struggling to stay afloat. When an extra-large wave lifted it up, he saw it clearly.

It was a horse, a black horse with something tangled around its neck.

"I see it!" he said.

The Ghost Girl didn't bother to answer. She was already scrambling down through the fuselage. Flip followed her. By the time he reached the ground, she'd crossed the clearing and was slipping into the tunnel. When he stepped into the open air on the far side, she was in the distance, running as fast as her thin little legs would take her.

Toward the beach, and the horse.

9 * *A Horse in the Waves*

THROUGH THE TREES and up the dunes the Ghost Girl ran, scampering over the sand like a goat. When Flip reached the top, she was on the beach. Without looking back to see whether he was behind her, she dashed straight to the water's edge and stood staring at the creature struggling in the waves.

It was a large horse, black from head to tail, with massive hooves, thick legs, and a neck almost as big as Flip's entire body. It was bobbing up and down in the water, kicking and bucking to stay afloat. As he watched, a wave crashed against its shoulders and it vanished in a mass of foam. A second later it reemerged, eyes wide with fear, its long mane plastered across its skull, water streaming from its nostrils.

Now he could see what was tangled around its neck and right leg: a clump of ropes and metal cables, waterlogged and heavy and dragging it down. If they weren't removed, the horse would drown before it reached the shore.

Flip's heart sank. He didn't have a knife, so he couldn't save the animal even if he wanted to. He couldn't even swim out to it because he didn't know how to swim. There was nothing he could do.

Or at least, that's what he thought until the Ghost Girl plucked a penknife from a pocket in her dress, snapped it open, and ran straight into the sea.

10 * *Rescued*

She didn't get far. The first wave struck her in the chest and knocked her down. A second wave submerged her completely.

Flip dashed into the surf, grabbed her by the collar, and pulled her back onto the sand. Coughing and spluttering, she jumped to her feet and ran straight back into the water. A fresh wave sent her spinning head over heels to where she'd started.

Out in the sea, the horse was still kicking and thrashing. But it was much weaker now, and moving more slowly. Two waves crashed into the back of its head and it sank from sight, only to break through to the surface seconds later, snorting water and shaking its head wildly from side to side.

The Ghost Girl grabbed Flip's hand and slapped the penknife into it. She pointed at the horse.

Flip knew what she meant, but he shook his head. "I can't!" he yelled above the roar of the wind. "I don't know what to do!"

She mimed cutting and pointed at the horse.

"I can't swim!" he said.

But even as he spoke, he knew he couldn't just stand there and do nothing. He could see the fear in the horse's eyes and he knew what that was like, to feel lost and alone, wondering where the people were who would take care of him. He'd felt that so many times in Amsterdam in the days after his mom left. And then in the months and years that followed, when his dad had gone out and he'd woken up in the middle of the night, all by himself in the dark, damp apartment. Swim or not, he couldn't just leave the horse to its fate.

Wrapping his fingers around the knife, Flip took a long deep breath and ran into the sea.

It was so cold it made him gasp. The moment he did so, a wave smacked him in the face and he swallowed a mouthful of seawater. He coughed and spat it out and while he was doing that, another wave did the same thing again. The knife was torn from his fingers and went spinning away before he could grab it. But he kept going, digging his feet hard into the sand and pushing himself forward against the current.

And then there wasn't any sand anymore.

He was swimming.

Or at least, not sinking. Up and down in the water he went, flailing with his legs, thrashing with his arms. A wave lifted him up. A second submerged him. A third, a fourth, and a fifth wave battered him about like a cork. Then, just as he was thinking he'd never make it, his fingers brushed against a strand of long coarse hair. It was the horse's mane. He clutched it tight, hauled himself forward, and locked his arms around the terrified animal's neck.

It reared upward, bellowing with fear, but Flip held fast, bouncing back and forth against its massive shoulders like a Ping-Pong ball against a paddle. When the horse twisted its head around, Flip could feel its hot, wet breath against his face.

Without thinking, he reached out and placed his hand on its muzzle, directly above its nostrils. For just a few seconds, the creature calmed. Its breathing slowed and its eyes grew less fearful.

Clutching the mane tight, Flip studied the knotted cables and oily rope around the horse's neck. Up close he could see they'd gotten caught in the leather halter it was wearing, as well as around its leg. That was why every kick dragged its head down. If he could get the halter off, perhaps the cables and rope would just fall away.

It was fastened with two straps: one around the muzzle and one behind the ears. He reached out and unbuckled the strap around the muzzle. He'd been right. The ropes loosened a little.

He reached for the strap behind the ears, only for a wave to hit him in the face and almost sweep him away from the horse. He scrambled for it again, but the waves kept knocking him away. Desperate now, he did the only thing he thought would work. He hauled himself forward and slid up onto the horse's back.

The extra weight immediately pushed it down in the water. Now the waves were breaking over its head and it thrashed blindly in panic. Grimly determined, Flip thrust his left hand under the leather strap and, with the fingers of his right hand turning white from the cold water, worked the second buckle loose.

Instantly, the halter came apart and the ropes and cables dropped beneath the waves. Finally free, the horse reared up. Water sluiced from its mane and back. Then it crashed back down and started swimming the last few feet to safety.

But as it surged forward, Flip flew backward. Before he could get his bearings or catch his breath, the waves had driven him under the surface and into the sand. His forehead smacked into something hard. He swallowed mouthfuls of water as he was tumbled upside down and hurled onto the shore.

When he opened his eyes, he was lying facedown on the beach with the surf breaking around his shoulders. The Ghost Girl had dropped to her knees beside him and was peering into his face. Totally exhausted, all he could do was stare back. And every few seconds cough and spit out what felt like gallons of seawater.

After a while he pushed himself upright and looked over at the horse. It was standing some distance away with its head down and sides heaving as its breathing returned to normal. Then it looked up and shook itself, sending water cascading from its mane and tail and coat.

Flip laughed. He couldn't help it.

He was alive.

All *three* of them were alive and he'd never felt so happy in his entire life.

11 * A New Friend

When Flip finally found the strength to sit up, he realized it wasn't raining anymore and that the wind had dropped. He got to his feet and looked at the horse. Then he looked at the Ghost Girl.

"What do we do now?" he asked.

She pointed at the village.

Of course, he thought. Somebody there would know what to do. He would turn the horse over to them. But when he reached out his hand to grab its mane, it shied away and snatched back its head. The sudden movement made Flip step back in alarm and this scared the horse even more. It turned and galloped off, stopping twenty paces away and turning to stare at the two children, letting out little snorts of fear every few seconds.

Flip's heart was thumping. He hadn't expected this. And now, safely out of the sea, he realized for the first time how tall the horse was, and how much bigger than him. If it had galloped *toward* him, it would have knocked him flat in a second.

Shivering, Flip crouched down on the sand, hugging himself and his wet clothes against the cold, trying to keep warm and think of a solution to the problem. A sound made him look up. The horse was approaching, head down, sniffing the air, moving one hoof at a time.

Flip stayed exactly where he was, ignoring the pain in his cramped leg muscles, not wanting to frighten the animal again. Finally, it stood right before him and lowered its massive head to sniff at his face and fingers. Flip felt a little nervous, but as gently as he could, he reached out and rested one hand on its muzzle. The horse didn't shy away.

Carefully—as carefully as the horse had come back to him—he stood up and ran his hand along its neck. It snorted with pleasure and shook its long mane from side to side. Flip shifted slowly, then stroked its muzzle. The horse let out a sigh and, a little while later, when Flip wrapped his hand in its mane, it didn't object at all. It turned and strolled along beside the boy without a murmur, hooves thumping softly on the sand.

The Ghost Girl came too, but she still wouldn't talk. Every question Flip asked her—her name, where she lived, what she was doing on the island—she answered with a blank stare and a shake of her head.

When they reached the village, the first thing they saw was the lifeboat, making its way up from the sea. The horses hauling it were wet from the rain and the waves but looked strong and lively and determined. Not so the lifeboat men, or Mr. Bouten in the cart at the rear of the column. They all looked tired and downcast. The villagers who came out to see them took one look at their faces and fell silent themselves. When one of them asked a question, Uncle Andries just shook his head.

Then he looked up, stopped walking and stared.

As long as he lived, Flip would never forget the look on the faces of the villagers as they turned to see what had caught Uncle Andries's attention. He didn't think he could have astonished them more if he'd grown wings and flown around the church tower. To add to it all, he could hear voices here and there muttering, "It's the boy from *Amsterdam*."

Then a voice boomed out from the back of the crowd. "What have you got there?"

A cigar-smoking figure pushed its way forward. Flip knew instantly who he was because he had the same short haircut and the same peglike ears as his three sons. It was Mr. Mesman, the owner of the hotel.

He was obviously a man used to taking charge. He strode forward and reached out his hand to take hold of the horse. But the moment he did so, it let out a whinny, shook its head violently from side to side, and took three steps back. Its hooves smacked against the surface of the road with a crack that froze Mr. Mesman in his tracks.

Flip stepped between the hotel owner and the frightened animal. Slowly, he turned around and held out his hands for the horse to sniff. He put one hand on its muzzle, the other on its neck. Gradually, its breathing slowed and its head sank down until the bottom of its muzzle rested on Flip's shoulder. But it never took its wary eyes off the villagers.

Or Mr. Mesman.

Uncle Andries stepped forward, but when he saw the alarm in the horse's eyes as he approached, he stopped and stood still.

"Why don't you tell us what happened?" he said.

So Flip did. He didn't mention being chased by the Mesman Boys. And he didn't say anything about the Ghost Girl being up in the rear turret of the bomber. When he looked around to see if she would confirm his story, he saw she'd vanished, as silently as ever.

"You didn't see where it came from?" Uncle Andries

asked when Flip finished. "There wasn't a boat anywhere? A ship?"

Flip shook his head.

"You're sure about that?"

"Positive," Flip said.

Uncle Andries turned to look at the other lifeboat men. One of them nodded. Uncle Andries turned back.

"The boat we went to rescue was carrying horses," he said. "But we couldn't save anybody. Or the horses. We were too late." Then he nodded at Flip's horse. "It looks like this one escaped and swam for the shore. And *you* rescued it." He gave Flip a curious look. "Can you swim?" he asked.

Flip shook his head.

"But you went into the water anyway?"

"I had to," Flip said.

"Why?"

"Because if I hadn't, the horse would have drowned," Flip said.

That was when something changed in the way his uncle looked at him. But Flip didn't get the chance to work out quite what it was because Mr. Mesman went over to Mr. Bouten's cart and snatched up a halter from behind the seat.

"Right," he said, "we'll take it from here."

"Take it where?" Uncle Andries asked.

"Somewhere safe, of course," Mr. Mesman said. "Until we find out who it belongs to."

"The mayor decides that," Uncle Andries said. "That's the law."

"The mayor isn't here today!" said Mr. Mesman. "He's gone to the mainland."

"Then we'll let Flip decide. He—"

"He's just a boy," Mr. Mesman barked. "From *Amsterdam*. What does *he* know about these things?"

The voices were scaring the horse. Its nostrils were flaring, and its ears were flicking nervously back and forth.

"Not much," Uncle Andries replied, lowering his voice when he saw the effect it was having on the animal. "But he rescued it. So until the mayor decides what's to become of it, I say Flip says where it stays."

"You don't own this island, you know," Mr. Mesman said, still talking as loudly as ever.

"And neither do you!" Uncle Andries replied, looking the hotel owner directly in the eye. "Not yet, anyway."

Flip noticed several of the villagers, as well as Mr. Bouten and the lifeboat crew, nodding in agreement. Mr. Mesman saw it too.

"All right!" he said, hurling the halter to the ground. "*You* take him!"

This time the horse did break loose. Shaking its head and snorting, it backed up against a fence behind it and knocked down a line of parked bicycles. It took Flip more than a minute to calm the animal down, stroking its shoulders and up the side of its neck, pressing his body against its side to reassure it.

Totally oblivious to the damage he'd just helped cause, Mr. Mesman stormed off with his hands in his pockets, puffing furiously on his cigar.

The street began to empty both of villagers and of the few curious vacationers who'd stopped to see what was going on. Uncle Andries said he'd see the lifeboat back safely to its house if Mr. Bouten would escort Flip and the horse to the farm. When the boat rumbled away, the old man bent down, picked up the halter, and held it out toward Flip. He'd seen what happened with strangers and didn't try to come closer.

But when Flip took the halter, the horse reared back. Flip stopped. He waited a few seconds and took a step forward. Again it reared back. Flip stood still, his heart pounding, his stomach fluttering with anxiety. What was wrong now? What was he supposed to do?

As if he could read the boy's thoughts, Mr. Bouten spoke up. "You're doing fine, Flip," he said. "Don't you worry about that. You're doing just fine with him."

Encouraged, Flip tried a third time, only to step back fast as the horse flinched once more and cracked its front hooves hard on the road.

"Something's bothering him," said Flip. "He won't let me put the halter on."

"I'm not sure what it is," said Mr. Bouten. "He should be used to it by now. But why don't you just drop it on the ground for now and lead him home the way you led him here. He doesn't seem to mind that."

So that's what Flip did. Taking hold of the horse's mane, he turned him away from the village and began to walk slowly in the direction of the farm. Mr. Bouten went with them, but made sure to stay at a safe distance.

"Looks to me, Flip," he said after a few minutes had passed with no further upsets, "like you've just made yourself a new friend."

12 * *Lover of Horses*

"Do you know anything about horses?" Mr. Bouten asked as they strolled along toward the farm. "You've certainly got a way with them."

Flip shook his head. "I've seen them pulling carts in Amsterdam," he said. "But that's all."

"Well, you'd never know that, now, would you?" Mr. Bouten said. "Not from the way he treats you. Perhaps it's your name."

"My name?" Flip asked. "What's wrong with it?"

"Nothing at all," Mr. Bouten said. "Don't you know what it means? Flip?"

"No. It was my mom who chose it."

"It's short for *Fillipus*. That's Greek. It means 'lover of horses.' Did she like horses?"

"She did," Flip said. "But she never got the chance to ride them. We never had enough money for that."

"Well," Mr. Bouten said, nodding at the creature as it plodded along, "perhaps he senses that. Horses are good at sensing things."

Flip had never been this close to an animal in his life—not a cat or a dog, or even a guinea pig at school—and he didn't know the first thing about them. Which was why he still couldn't get over how much this one seemed to like him. Or Mr. Bouten saying he had a way with horses. That *really* surprised him.

"They are?" he asked.

"Comes from when they lived out in the wild," Mr. Bouten said. "If they wanted to stay alive, they had to be able to notice even the *slightest* change in their surroundings. And when they did, off they'd go, as fast as they could on those big long horse legs of theirs, away from whatever was trying to hurt them."

"But *you* don't want to hurt him," Flip said.

"No, I don't."

"Then why won't he let you near him?"

Mr. Bouten smiled again. "Because there's no telling what a horse'll decide to be scared of. They're also very *unpredictable* creatures."

Flip shook his head, puzzled.

Mr. Bouten explained. "Say you're walking down the road and you see a scrap of paper blowing along the ground. You think, *Oh, there's a scrap of paper blowing along the ground*, and you don't take any more notice of it. But a horse doesn't know it's a scrap of paper. It just thinks, *I haven't seen that there before. Perhaps it's going to attack me!* And off it goes at a gallop. Or jumps sideways. Or turns around and runs back the way it came. Reason I limp like this is because of a horse that got scared."

"A horse?" Flip said.

Mr. Bouten nodded. "A young mare she was. Anja. I used to ride her everywhere on the island. One day I was out late, after dark in the winter, and we were going home past the churchyard. There was a wind blowing, but I didn't take any notice of that. Or the creaking branch. It was a big branch too, swaying back and forth, just about ready to break. *I* didn't pay it no mind, but Anja did, and she didn't like it. Kept trying to get away. I ignored her, though. I made her keep walking." Mr. Bouten shook his head at the memory. "And when that branch *did* break, she bolted."

"What happened?" Flip said.

"She went one way—and I went the other. Flew right out of the saddle like my backside was made of butter and landed with my leg bent up under me and broken in three places. Nobody found me until the next morning. By which time my leg was in a right mess."

"Couldn't they fix it?"

"Oh, they tried," Mr. Bouten said. "But they had to take me to the mainland, which was a *long* journey in them days—1938 it was, before the war, and the roads weren't anything like as good as they are now. By the time I got to the hospital, my bones were in a terrible state. The doctors did their best, but they never could get everything straightened out properly. I've been limping ever since."

"What happened to Anja?"

"Nothing."

"But she hurt you," Flip said.

Mr. Bouten disagreed. "She was just being a horse," he said. "She *knew* something was wrong in that churchyard. She could *hear* the tree wasn't right. It was *me* what wasn't paying attention. That's when I learned it's usually a good idea to pay attention to animals. And I have done so ever since."

By now they'd reached the farm. Aunt Elly and Renske were waiting outside. Flip told them both what had happened. When he was finished, Renske went toward the horse, only to stop abruptly when he backed away in fright at her approach.

"Doesn't he like me?" she asked. "Is he scared of me?"

"I think he's scared of everyone," Flip said. "Not just you."

But that didn't help. Renske walked sadly back to her mother. "I'm only seven," she muttered. "Nobody's scared of you when you're *seven*."

Flip looked at the horse. Then at Renske. She looked so disappointed that he went over to her, took her hand, and walked her slowly back. The horse snorted, but let the children approach. When they were close enough to touch, Flip made Renske stand still while he counted silently up to sixty. Then he lifted her hand in his so the horse could smell them both at the same time. After counting to thirty, he very gently slid his hand away from hers and stepped back to leave them alone. This time the horse made no complaint—he even blew on Renske's fingers, which made her giggle.

"What kind of horse is he?" she asked.

"He's a Friesian," Mr. Bouten said.

"That's here," she said. "Friesland."

"Yes," Mr. Bouten said. "This part of the country's where he comes from. Smart, Friesians are. Strong too. Good horses." Then he pointed at the spot where the ropes and the wire had dragged and rubbed against the skin. They'd left a shallow ragged gash the size of Flip's hand. "We need to fix that," he said. "But we'll clean him up and give him some food first. And before we do that, we'll make him a nice warm bed to lie down on for when we're finished. After everything he's been through, he must be absolutely exhausted."

Flip led the horse into the barn and helped Mr. Bouten scatter a thick layer of straw in one of the horse stalls. Then they gave the horse a drink of water.

"But not too much, mind," Mr. Bouten said. "Don't want him to get colic."

"What's that?" Flip asked.

Mr. Bouten thought for a second or two. "A really, really bad bellyache," he said. "That's the simplest way to describe it. Probably doesn't sound so bad to you, but it's serious for a horse. You don't want your horse to get colic if you can help it."

He handed Flip an old towel and told him how to rub the animal down and get him as clean as possible. When he finished, Mr. Bouten mixed up some oats and water in a bucket, added a spoonful of cod-liver oil, and placed it on the ground. The horse polished it off in seconds.

"Good appetite," he said.

He filled a net with hay, hung it up high on a hook on the wall inside the stall, and stepped aside to let Flip lead the horse in. Then he fetched some warm salty water and, while the horse munched happily on the hay, he instructed Flip how to clean the wound left by the ropes and cables.

"And *now*," he said, sliding the bolt on the stable door, "we'll leave him alone and let him get some rest."

"Can't we stay and watch him?" Renske said, a second before Flip asked exactly the same thing.

Mr. Bouten shook his head. "He needs his rest. And the best way for him to get that is to leave him on his own. Give him a chance to relax. I think he'd appreciate that."

"What's going to happen to him?" Renske asked as they all walked back to the house.

"Oh, the owners'll come and fetch him, I expect," Mr. Bouten said. "Soon as they find out he's missing."

When he heard that, Flip stopped and glanced back into the barn at the horse. He was still looking forward to leaving the island. He still wanted his mom to come and get him so they could go. But he couldn't get over how the horse had looked to *him* for protection. How he had let only *him* stay close in the village.

Nobody had ever wanted Flip to look after them before. Not at school. Not at home. But the horse had. The horse had turned to Flip for help. And he'd liked helping him.

He hoped he could go on helping him until the owner appeared. That, he thought, might be fun.

13 * A Dawn Conversation

By now, Flip had grown used to waking up at dawn, when Uncle Andries brought the cows in for milking. But the morning after he rescued the horse, he was awake even earlier, while it was still dark. He could hear something banging down below in the barn. Dressing as quickly as he could, he went downstairs and realized that it was the Friesian, kicking at the stall door with a front hoof.

The horse's head loomed out of the shadows as Flip approached. He gave a little nicker of recognition and let Flip stroke his muzzle.

"Hello," Flip whispered. "What do *you* want?"

The horse proceeded to rub his muzzle against Flip's hands and up under his arms. Flip laughed. He couldn't help it. The horse went on poking and rubbing with his muzzle.

"Of course," he said, finally understanding. "You want something to eat."

He realized he was talking out loud, which was silly because an animal couldn't understand him. Feeling embarrassed, he glanced over his shoulder to see if anybody had heard him. But he also couldn't help noticing that the horse had calmed down and pricked his ears up with each word he spoke.

"I don't know how much food to give you," he said.

The horse stared down at him and again banged his hoof against the stall door.

"I really don't," Flip said.

All at once he remembered Mr. Bouten filling the net with hay the day before and decided it couldn't hurt to do the same. He reached in and untied the net, then filled it again and hung it up from the hook beside the door. By then the first faint traces of sunlight were breaking over the horizon and shining through a dusty window in the rear wall of the barn. He stood back and watched as the Friesian began to eat.

It was quiet inside, and peaceful. Flip liked the silence.

When the horse had finished and was licking his lips to get every last scrap of enjoyment out of the hay, Flip reached up to take away the net. As he did so, the letter from his mom—the one he'd folded up for safe-keeping between two sheets of cardboard—rode up out of his pants pocket. The horse saw it and promptly tried to eat it.

Flip jumped back. "You can't have *that*!"

The words came out louder than he'd intended and the horse pulled away. He stood at the back of the stall, scared, ears flicking.

"It's from my mom," Flip explained quietly, sliding the letter safely back into his pocket. "It's the last thing she ever wrote to me. It's almost all I've got left of her."

The horse walked cautiously back toward him. Flip climbed up to perch on the edge of the stall.

"Sorry," he said. "I shouldn't have shouted."

The horse poked his head over the door and looked around the barn.

"I wish I knew what to do with you," Flip said. "My mom probably would. She liked horses. She always stopped when they rode past in Amsterdam, especially the ones the policemen rode. She said they were beautiful. I bet she'd like you."

The horse was now standing with his head resting against Flip's arm. Flip scratched his muzzle. His voice really did seem to calm the animal down, so he went on talking. And the more he did, the more he enjoyed it. He didn't feel silly at all.

"That was nice what you did yesterday," he said. "For Renske. Letting her be your friend."

The horse looked into Flip's eyes.

"I think you like the Ghost Girl too," Flip went on. "She's the other girl. She was with me on the beach. Except you never know when you're going to see her. Oh, and I'm Flip, by the way. That's my name. Just so you know."

The horse let out a little snort and twitched his ears.

"Flip," Flip repeated.

The horse lifted his muzzle and snorted a jet of warm air right into Flip's face.

"I like you too," he laughed. And then he grew serious. "I wonder where you come from," he said. "What your home's like. And your owner. It must be fun to look after a horse."

Abruptly, the horse swung around to face the entrance to the barn. Flip looked up to see Mr. Bouten standing there, ready to bring the cows in for milking.

"Hello," the old man said. "*You're* up early."

"Yes," Flip replied, feeling awkward, wondering if Mr. Bouten had heard him talking. "I gave him some hay," he said, hoping to change the subject. "I filled the net, like you did yesterday, hung it up just like you did. I hope I didn't give him too much."

"Not at all," Mr. Bouten said. "Just the thing for him. Well done. I heard you talking to him, by the way," he continued. Now Flip *really* felt awkward. But the feeling vanished as Mr. Bouten came closer. "Good for you," he said. "They like the sound of a friendly voice."

"They do?"

"Oh yes," Mr. Bouten said. "It's always a good idea to talk to horses. Helps them relax. Did someone teach you that?"

"No," Flip said. "It just seemed like the right thing to do."

Mr. Bouten smiled. "See," he said. "I was right."

"About what?" Flip asked.

"You," Mr. Bouten said. "You *do* have a way with horses."

And the horse let out another long snort and rubbed his muzzle up and down against Flip's back, as if he were nodding his agreement.

14 * A New Name

FOR THE NEXT three days, a lot of people spent a lot of time trying to find out who the horse belonged to. The mayor made telephone calls. The vicar got in touch with his colleagues on the other islands. The police came over from the mainland, followed by two insurance company men in suits and hats, carrying big briefcases. They marched all over Mossum, taking notes.

All any of them managed to do was identify the man whose boat had sunk the day the horse arrived on the island. He was a farmer who'd lived alone on an island to the east. He'd had no family. He'd had no friends. The man he'd been going to visit on Vlieland, an island to the west, had agreed to buy three horses. But he hadn't agreed to buy a black Friesian. The farmer on Vlieland didn't know anything at *all* about a black Friesian gelding.

To make matters even more complicated, when the insurance men in suits and hats and big briefcases finally visited the dead man's home, they found a dilapidated farmhouse crammed from kitchen to bedrooms with all kinds of indescribable junk. Yet nowhere in any of that junk was a single mention of any horse even vaguely resembling the one Flip had rescued.

There was no proof he'd ever belonged to anybody. So what was to happen with him? The mayor of Mossum, Mr. Balkensten, paid a trip to the farm to explain. He started speaking in Fries to the grown-ups until Aunt Elly stopped him. She pointed out that since Flip had rescued the horse, he should be able to listen as well. The mayor looked puzzled, as if worrying about what children thought was silly. But he did what she asked.

It was a strange case, he said. By law, anything that washed up on shore had to be reported to him. *He* then decided what happened to it. If it wasn't worth anything, he usually let the finder keep it. If it was a valuable item, he arranged a public auction in conjunction with the insurance company and saw that the proceeds were split appropriately.

None of that, however, helped with the horse. It was definitely valuable; it was after all a sound, healthy

Friesian. But there was no record of its existence. Nobody could prove they owned it. The only person who could have done so had drowned when his boat sank.

"So what *I* think," said the mayor, "is that we treat it as lost property. Whoever finds something keeps it for a year. If nobody comes forward to claim it during that time, then it will belong to the person who found it."

"Which is Flip," Aunt Elly said.

"Well, yes," said the mayor. "But seeing as how he's a minor, I think nobody would argue with me were I to say that I think it should go to Mr. Bor, the boy's uncle."

"But I don't *want* another horse," Uncle Andries said. "There's only enough work for Leila. There's nothing for another horse to do."

"I quite understand," the mayor said. "And I wouldn't dream of forcing you to take it. But I don't think it'll be a problem. I'm fairly certain I can find another home for it."

Uncle Andries looked up. "You can? I don't know anybody on Mossum who needs a new horse. Keeping a horse is expensive and there's not that much money on the island."

"I know someone," Mr. Bouten said quietly.

Everyone turned to look at him.

"Mr. Mesman. He'd find a use for it."

The mayor nodded. "He *has* expressed an interest," he said.

"But he *can't*! You can't let him go *there*!"

It was Flip who'd spoken. Practically shouted. Now everyone in the room turned to look at him.

Uncle Andries was furious. "How *dare* you speak to the mayor like that!" he said. "Apologize this second!"

Flip felt himself blushing as he said, "I'm sorry." But then he couldn't stop himself from adding, "You really *can't* give the horse to Mr. Mesman!"

"That's *enough*!" Uncle Andries snapped. He turned to the mayor. "If you don't mind, sir, I'd like a word with my nephew. In private."

"Of course," the mayor said, and stepped outside.

Uncle Andries turned to Flip. "How *dare* you talk to him like that? Is that how you talked back in Amsterdam?"

Flip shook his head. Actually, he'd never talked back to *anyone* in Amsterdam. Certainly not grown-ups. His dad had never allowed it and nobody did it at school with the teachers. He hadn't wanted to do it now, either, but he just couldn't keep quiet.

"The mayor is the queen's representative on this island," Uncle Andries said, "and you'll treat him with the respect his position deserves. Is that quite clear?"

"Yes," Flip said.

"I certainly hope so." Uncle Andries stared at him for a moment, then leaned back in his chair. "Now," he said quietly, "*why* can't Mr. Mesman have the Friesian?"

For the last three days, Flip had helped feed the horse and brush him, tending to his wounds, and he'd enjoyed every single moment. The thought of not being able to go on doing that was awful. The thought of him going to the Mesmans was even worse. And he didn't like the way the mayor kept calling the horse *it*.

"Because I don't think he'd look after him," he said. "And all his sons do is kill birds with their slingshots. They *definitely* wouldn't look after him. Not properly. I just know they wouldn't."

"Those three are terrors when it comes to animals," Mr. Bouten agreed. "I can't see them looking after one to save their lives."

"Nor their father," Aunt Elly added. "I think he just wants to own the horse. Like he wants to own the island. And even if he didn't hurt it on purpose, he'd end up doing just that because he wouldn't know any different."

Uncle Andries nodded slowly. "I can't argue with a single word of that," he said at last. "But the horse can't stay here because I haven't got the time to look after it. And that's all there is to it."

"Then let me," Flip said. "Let *me* look after him."

His aunt and his uncle were astonished. "*You?*" they said in unison.

"Yes," Flip said. "Me."

Uncle Andries shook his head. "No," he said. "Out of the question."

But Flip wasn't going to give up. He couldn't. For his sake. And more importantly, for the horse's. "I know I can. Ask Mr. Bouten. He said I have a way with horses."

Mr. Bouten smiled. "I did," he said. "I've seen him. The boy's a natural."

"But he doesn't know anything *about* them," Uncle Andries said.

"He'll learn," Mr. Bouten replied. "If you give him the chance. And I bet he'll learn quicker than most."

"Are you sure about that, Hendrick?" Uncle Andries asked.

"Yes," Mr. Bouten replied, looking calmly back at Uncle Andries. "I am."

Uncle Andries scratched his head. "Well, it's summer, which means there's plenty of grass in the field. Enough for him and Leila. But what about when winter comes? How do we pay for him then?"

"Probably won't be here by then," Mr. Bouten said. "Somebody's bound to turn up *eventually* and claim him, good horse like that. But until that day comes, I say let the boy look after him."

Uncle Andries turned to Aunt Elly. She thought about it for a while, then slowly nodded her agreement.

"All right," Uncle Andries said. "The horse can stay here."

Flip could hardly believe his ears.

"*But,*" Uncle Andries continued, "it'll all be up to you. Not me. Not Mr. Bouten. Not your aunt. *You* will be responsible for that horse and for everything it does. I hope you understand that."

"I do," Flip said. "And I will. I promise."

"And I won't have it interfering with your work here on the farm. Do you understand that too?"

Flip was too excited to speak, so all he did was nod.

"Then," said Uncle Andries, getting up from his chair, "I'll go and tell the mayor."

The mayor listened to his decision, said that would be fine, and set off back to the village. Flip went straight out to the barn to see the horse. Renske followed him.

"He'll have to have a name," she said. "Otherwise he won't know who we're talking to when we talk to him."

"What if he already has a name?" Flip said. "He won't recognize a new one."

"Oh no," Renske said, shaking her head. "He'll soon learn it. Horses are clever. And *you* have to name him because *you* saved him. I'm sure that's what he's expecting."

Flip leaned on the stable door, thinking. It didn't take him long.

"Then I'll call him Storm," he said. "Because that's where he came from."

The horse looked up and snorted. He stuck his head over the stable door and let the children scratch his muzzle.

"See," Renske said. "He likes it. He thinks it's a good name too."

What neither of them realized was that it was a name Storm would more than live up to.

15 * *Too Much Energy*

The morning after the mayor's visit, Mr. Bouten inspected the wound on Storm's shoulder, and announced that it was healed and that he was ready to go out into the field with Leila.

"But first," he added, producing a box of brushes, currycombs, and hoof-picks, "we'll give him an extra-good clean."

Flip liked grooming, but it was hard work. Harder than he'd expected. Working the brush over the broad chest and flanks, smoothing the knots out of Storm's mane and tail, getting him to lift his great big hooves up off the ground so they could be cleaned took all Flip's energy. He ended up with aching arms and sweat dripping from his forehead.

But he loved being next to the horse, feeling the warmth of his coat and listening to his slow, steady breathing. And he loved seeing how the brushing and combing made Storm's coal-black coat practically gleam. He knew Storm liked it too, because when he was with him in the stall, the horse calmed down, stood still, and acted as if there was no other place he'd rather be.

So it was a little disappointing that the moment Flip and Renske led him out to the field to join Leila, Storm took one look at the other horse and trotted across the grass toward her. He didn't look back or even hesitate.

"Don't worry," Mr. Bouten said when he saw Flip's expression. "He hasn't forgotten you. He'll be back. But right now he's got a horse friend to make."

Out in the middle of the field, Storm slowed and began examining his new surroundings, flicking his ears, sniffing the air for signs of danger. Leila was doing the same. The two horses walked slowly forward, tails swishing, each taking cautious sniffs of the other.

Then Leila put her head down and, with a little squeal, kicked up her hind legs and started to gallop. Storm set off after her. For the next ten minutes, the two horses raced furiously back and forth, Storm in the lead, Leila following, clods of mud and grass flying up from their hooves in all directions.

"What are they doing?" Flip asked.

"Working out who's in charge," Mr. Bouten said.

"And then what?" Flip asked.

"Oh," Mr. Bouten said, "once that's all sorted out, they can be friends. They can relax."

"How will they know who is?" Flip asked. "In charge?"

"The one behind's the one in charge, telling the horse in front to keep going." He smiled. "And this is Leila's field. So she's not going to let anyone come in here and tell *her* what to do."

Eventually, Leila slowed her pace and ambled over to the water trough for a long refreshing drink.

Storm followed, breathing hard and shaking his head. When Leila had finished, he took a drink as well. Then he sank to his knees in a patch of muddy grass and rolled onto his back. Almost immediately, he jumped back up and took a quick look around. Satisfied that he was safe, he lay back down and went on happily rolling.

As they stood watching, Flip sensed movement beside him and turned to see the Ghost Girl step silently up to the gate. She didn't look at him, or at Renske or Mr. Bouten. All her concentration was focused on Storm.

When he clambered back to his feet his mane was tangled, his tail was knotted, and there were mud and grass stains on his legs and flanks. He looked worse than he had the day he'd emerged from the sea. There was little trace left of the gleaming black coat he'd gone into the field with. The Ghost Girl giggled.

It was the first sound Flip had ever heard her make and, like Renske, all he could do was stare, wide-eyed with surprise. The girl ignored them and giggled again. When she giggled a third time, Renske joined in. And that eventually made Flip smile. It was only dirt, he thought. He'd just brush it away the next time he cleaned Storm.

But his smile vanished when he looked up to see the Friesian was now busy looking for ways to escape. It had taken him practically no time at all to spot a gap in the hedge at the far end of the field, closed off with three old wooden boards. The boards had always kept Leila in, but to Storm they were nothing more than a minor inconvenience. He nudged them with his nose until they came loose and fell to the ground, then he strolled into the next-door field to begin grazing happily on the lush new grass it contained.

Flip followed him and guided him gently back through the gap. Then he helped Mr. Bouten close it off properly. But no sooner had they finished than Storm was off again, pushing his way through a tangle of weeds and bushes at the base of a tree on the other side of the field.

Flip went after him a second time, led him back, and held tight to his mane while Mr. Bouten fetched an old wooden door from the barn and jammed it upright between the bushes.

Flip couldn't help feeling disappointed. First, Storm had trotted off the moment he saw Leila. Now it looked like he was trying to get away from the farm. And from the people who'd rescued him and looked after him.

"Why does he keep trying to escape?" he asked.

"Probably trying to see what he can get away with," Mr. Bouten said. "A horse brave enough to jump into the sea and try to swim to safety is bound to be independent."

Or perhaps he just wants to go home, Flip thought. *And be with whoever had looked after him.* Just like Flip wanted to be back with his mom. He could certainly understand that.

At lunchtime, he recounted everything that had happened.

"Too much energy," Uncle Andries said. The look on his face said he'd been expecting something like this. Clearly, he wasn't too happy about it.

"Well, why don't you give him a job to do?" Aunt Elly suggested. "Take his mind off things for a while? While he settles in."

Mr. Bouten agreed. "There's always that tree," he said.

In the far corner of one of the farm's fields, a tree had been struck by lightning a month before Flip's arrival on Mossum. Ever since, it had lain where it fell, blocking a ditch and covering the remains of a gate it had smashed in its fall. Uncle Andries, who wanted the ditch unblocked and the gate rebuilt before winter, thought that Leila and Storm's combined strength could drag the tree free. That would let him complete the necessary repairs without having to spend hours sawing the trunk into pieces first—hours he didn't have to spare in the busy summer days.

So with Flip's help, the two men led Leila and Storm over to the barn to fit them into the harnesses required for pulling a heavy object. Storm stood patiently by while Leila was prepared, but the moment the ropes and harness came near him and *his* shoulders, he bucked and stamped his hooves and backed away until it was removed. No matter how carefully and patiently they tried, Storm refused to be harnessed. So, much to Uncle Andries's obvious irritation, back into the field the horses went.

"What about the lifeboat?" Flip asked.

Mr. Bouten shook his head. "If he's like that here, think what he'd be like there. He panics and starts kicking with those big hooves of his, no telling what damage he'll do. To the horses *and* the boat. No, we can't have that."

"Can't you train him?" Flip asked.

"More than likely," Mr. Bouten said. "But that takes time."

"And this is summer," Uncle Andries broke in. "We've got more than enough to do on the farm." Not bothering to hide his frustration, he strode off back to work.

Flip walked over to the gate and watched the two horses trotting around the field, snorting and squealing and having the time of their lives. He couldn't understand why Storm was being so difficult. Or what he could to do to help him stop. All he could do was hope the horse would settle down and behave himself soon.

But worse was to come the next day.

16 * Brambles

IT ALL STARTED because Renske knew how Leila went to the bathroom.

It was just before lunch and she was sitting at one end of the gate, watching the two horses. The Ghost Girl, who'd once again appeared without a sound, was now sitting silently at the other end. Flip stood in between.

"She's a very clever horse," Renske said. "She always goes over to one side of the field."

Flip looked up. "Who does?" He'd just been into the field to say hello to Storm and was about to push the gate shut.

"Leila," Renske said. "When she needs to poop, she walks off to the side of the field and does it there. And since it's her field and she's in charge, Storm does too—to make sure *his* smell is there as well. I know. I've watched them."

As if to prove her point, Leila stopped eating, strolled over to the edge of the field, and left a pile of droppings. Then she walked back to the middle of the field and went on eating.

"What does she do that for?" Flip asked.

"So she doesn't poop on nice green grass to eat," Renske explained. "She makes sure to go in one place so she ruins as little grass as possible. Not like most horses, who go anywhere. Or cows. Cows do it wherever they're standing, which must be really annoying for all the other cows, because imagine if you're a cow and you're going to eat a nice bit of grass but you can't because your friend's just done her business all over it."

At the end of the gate, the Ghost Girl giggled.

"And sheep are just as bad!" Renske went on. "You can't walk through a sheep field or a cow field without getting your shoes covered in poop. That's why I like Leila. She looks after my shoes."

This time it wasn't just the Ghost Girl who giggled. Flip laughed too. That made the Ghost Girl giggle again. Then Renske joined in, and within seconds the three of them were laughing so hard the two girls had to climb down from the gate in case they fell off. This seemed even funnier, and soon the three of them were kneeling on the grass with aching sides and so many tears running down their faces they couldn't see a thing. They only stopped when Flip wiped his eyes, looked into the field, and asked, "Where's Storm?"

The gate was open.

Storm was nowhere in sight.

Renske and the Ghost Girl jumped to their feet. Flip clambered up onto the gatepost and peered in every direction. Far away at the end of the road that led to the village, he spotted Storm trotting happily along.

Oh no, he thought. His heart sank, not just because Storm had escaped yet again, but at the prospect of what Uncle Andries would say when he found out. Without a word, the three of them ran off in pursuit. And it *was* a pursuit, because every time they got close enough to grab him, Storm would just toss his head and twist away out of reach.

So they followed him along the road past the village, past the Hofstra farm, and then all the way down to The Eyes, two low-lying stretches of water on the southern side of the island. They found him at the far end of the farthest Eye, with his mane and his tail caught in a tangle of brambles clinging to the branches of a dead fallen tree he had tried to pick his way over. And he couldn't get loose.

The children tried their best to free him, but it was

no use. They weren't tall enough to reach him, or strong enough to break the branches. And the thorns ripped at their hands when they got too close. Storm was stuck.

With a sinking feeling in his stomach, Flip went to ask his uncle for help.

The news made Uncle Andries angry. He walked out to The Eyes with Aunt Elly and Mr. Bouten, put his hands in his overall pockets, and glared at the horse. "I'm beginning," he muttered, "to see why his last owner wanted to get rid of him. He's turning out to be more trouble than he's worth."

Flip felt awful. He'd promised to look after Storm and yet now, not even two days later, the horse was already in trouble again. To make him feel even worse, he could see the Mesman Boys on the far side of the water, laughing at all the chaos.

Eventually, the grown-ups managed to cut Storm free. But when Uncle Andries tried to loop a rope around his neck to lead him back to the farm, Storm bucked and whinnied with fear and galloped away out of reach.

Flip ran after him. He found the horse standing still by a stile in the path and led him back to the adults, holding gently to his mane.

But that didn't impress Uncle Andries.

"Your *horse*," he said, "either learns to behave, or somebody'd best come claim him before winter."

He strode off back to the farm with Aunt Elly at his side.

Flip turned to Mr. Bouten. "What did he mean?" he asked. "Before winter?"

"He means it's no good having a horse on a farm if it won't work. If Storm won't calm down and help with some work, he really will have to go somewhere else."

And that was when Flip finally understood. It all made sense. "The ropes!" he said. "And the harnesses. He was trapped in them in the sea and they almost drowned him. That's why they frighten him!"

"Then he'll have to learn not to be frightened," Mr. Bouten said.

"How does he do that?"

"Someone'll have to help him," Mr. Bouten said.

"Who?"

"You," said Mr. Bouten, as though it were the most obvious thing in the world.

"Me?"

"You want him to stay, don't you? You said you'd look after him."

"But I don't know how!" Flip said, scared at what was being asked of him. Nobody had ever said anything like this to him before. He'd never been encouraged to think for himself by his father. "What should I do?"

"I don't have *all* the answers," Mr. Bouten said, not unkindly. "But one thing occurs to me. He trusts you, doesn't he?"

Flip nodded.

"How did you do that? How did you get him to trust you so you could lead him into the village?"

Flip remembered how Storm had approached him after he had crouched down on the sand, and also how long it had taken before the horse had finally stopped beside him. "I didn't do anything, really. I just waited."

"And he realized you weren't going to hurt him. You were patient with him."

"Yes."

"Well, perhaps you should try being patient with the ropes and harness. Perhaps that would work."

"What if it doesn't?"

"You rescued him from the sea, Flip. You didn't know how to swim, but you went into the water and rescued him. If you can do that, you can do this."

He turned and limped away, leaving Flip staring up at Storm and Storm looking down at Flip. In the distance, the Mesman Boys were shouting that *they* could do a better job with the horse any day, but Flip didn't pay them any attention. He had other things to worry about. Slowly, he began walking Storm back to the farm.

Patient, he thought. And as he did so, a plan blossomed in his mind. *Yes*, he told himself, *I can be patient.*

17 * Day by Day

THE NEXT MORNING, Flip was awake and dressed and sitting on the gate to the horses' field before the sun had even broken over the horizon. Next to him, lying over the top bar of the gate, was a length of rope.

When the two horses trotted up to say hello, Storm saw the rope and stopped dead, sniffing the air. Flip sidled away to the other end of the gate. He didn't even look at the rope. He sat perfectly still with his hands by his sides.

"Hello," he said to the horses. "Did you sleep well? I did. After all that excitement yesterday."

He continued to ignore the rope. Gradually, Storm came closer. Soon he was sniffing at Flip's pockets, looking for food. Still talking, Flip gave each horse half a carrot, scratched their ears, and stroked their muzzles. Then he climbed down off the gate and started walking across the grass. He walked slowly, not looking back.

All he wanted right then was for Storm to follow him. Nothing more. As long as he got used to following Flip around the field, that would be enough for the moment.

And Storm did. Leila came too, for a few minutes at least. But when she stopped and wandered off on her own, Storm stayed with Flip, plodding quietly along after him. Up and down the field they went, three times in all, and all the time Flip chatted away to Storm about anything that came into his head: how cool it was outside, the sound the birds made in the trees, how the clouds in the distance looked like trees. Anything to keep the horse calm and feeling safe.

It worked. Storm remained docile. But when Flip reached the gate and lifted the rope off it, the horse backed away and watched from a distance. He clearly didn't like it.

Flip stayed still on the grass. "It's just a rope," he said. "It won't hurt you. I won't let it."

By then it was time for breakfast. He put the rope back on the gate and left it there all day. When he returned after work, it was still in place. He picked it up, draped it over his shoulders, and began walking around the field again. Storm followed, but from farther back this time. And he never got closer.

Flip didn't worry, though. He knew that what he wanted would take time to happen.

So the next day, he got up and did the same thing all over again.

And every day for the rest of the week.

By the seventh day, Storm was still nervous about the rope, but his trust in Flip was growing and he now walked quietly up and down the field beside him, letting Flip pat his shoulder and stroke his muzzle. When, on the eighth day, Flip laid one end of the rope carefully over the horse's shoulders, Storm didn't so much as snort.

But he still didn't like the harness.

And he hated the halter.

After his success with the rope, Flip started bringing a harness and a halter out to the field and placing them on the gate. But every time he saw them, Storm took one look and trotted away out of reach. He refused to come back, no matter what Flip did or said.

This went on for another week. At the beginning of the third week, the Mesman Boys decided it was time to tell Flip what to do. They strolled up to the gate, pushed it open, and walked into the field as though they owned it.

"You haven't got a clue, have you, city boy?" Jan said. "You don't *talk* to horses."

"They're just *animals*," Petrus said.

"You dump that harness on and *show* them who's boss!" Thijs said.

Flip was standing by the water trough. He turned away, held out his hand, and called to Storm. But the boys' shouting had scared the horse and he was keeping his distance.

"A good *slap's* what he needs," Petrus said. "Or a good crack with a whip."

"Not a lot of talking," Jan said.

Then all three boys laughed and shouted out together, "*City boy!*"

Suddenly furious, Flip spun around and ran toward them, only to stop when he saw Uncle Andries marching up the road with Mr. Bouten limping along behind.

"You three get *out* of my field *this minute*!" Uncle Andries roared.

For a moment, nobody moved. The obvious fury in the farmer's eyes froze all four boys with fear. Then the spell was broken. Clutching their slingshots and trophies, the Mesman Boys scuttled back to the road and away toward the village.

Uncle Andries watched them go and shook his head. In his hand he held a length of chain. He used it to close the gate and then added a padlock to keep it shut.

"I never thought I'd see the day I had to lock a gate on Mossum," he muttered.

"You can't blame Flip for those little thugs," Mr. Bouten said.

"I suppose not," Uncle Andries said. He didn't sound as though he believed it, though.

"And it's not Storm's fault, either," the older man said, quietly but firmly. "You know that."

This time, Uncle Andries didn't respond. He gave the key to the padlock to Flip, told him to make sure the gate was always closed and locked, and walked away.

Mr. Bouten patted Flip on the shoulder. "Don't you worry about him," he said. "He'll calm down." Then he pointed at the field. "You're doing well. I've been watching. I knew you could do it."

Flip wasn't sure he agreed. "But he won't come near the harness or the halter," he said. "He still hates *them*."

Mr. Bouten thought it over. "Tried a rope halter? He might let you fit that."

Flip didn't know what that was, so Mr. Bouten showed him. Using a length of light rope with a small noose at one end, they looped it up over Storm's ears and around his muzzle. Flip couldn't reach all the way, so, without thinking, Mr. Bouten placed the rope around the horse's ears. Storm wasn't frightened. He even turned his head to give the older man a friendly sniff.

"See," Mr. Bouten said, smiling. "You really *have* made a difference."

At that, Flip's whole body swelled with pride. He hadn't changed Storm completely, but he *had* made a difference. He really had. And not once had he used a whip like the Mesman Boys suggested.

"You should try taking him for a walk," Mr. Bouten said as Flip led Storm gently around the field. "The exercise'd do him good, and wearing that rope halter would probably get him used to the idea of a real one. And then, later on, a bridle. Ask your uncle. I'll back you up."

So Flip did, the next day at breakfast.

"If he really has got too much energy," he said, remembering his uncle's words that first day in the field, "walking would use it up. And the rope halter would get him used to a harness and a real halter."

Uncle Andries didn't reply.

"I'd only do it after all my other work," Flip continued. "And nobody would have to come with me. I'd do it all on my own. I really would. And it would just be walking."

"What harm could that do?" Aunt Elly asked. "Where could he go?"

"Probably straight into the nearest bramble bush," Uncle Andries said.

Then Mr. Bouten stepped in. "That's not fair, Andries," he said quietly. "Flip here's got Storm used to those ropes. *And* he's got him so he'd let me fit that halter, which is more than he did when he arrived. A sight more. He's done well, Flip has. Very well."

Uncle Andries drank his coffee in silence. He put down the cup. Then he stood up and looked across the table at Flip. "All right," he said. "I'll let you try."

Flip let out a sigh of relief.

"But," his uncle continued sternly, "it's still the same agreement. Storm's *your* responsibility. If anything goes wrong, it'll be down to you."

"It won't," Flip said, almost too excited to talk. "I promise it won't."

"It had better not," his uncle said as he left the kitchen.

18 * A Fading Face

Flip never forgot the days that followed.

They'd always begin the same. Well before dawn, with an apple or a carrot tucked into his pocket, he'd leave the barn, race over to the horses' field, and climb up onto the gate. The island would be completely still. The only sound would be the faint chatter and trill of birds in the trees. Then, out of the darkness Leila and Storm would come running, their hooves drumming on the soft ground, all the way up from the far end of the field to see if he'd brought them anything to eat.

After that, it was a stroll around the field with Storm until breakfast, always with the rope halter fitted. Then it was work, which was hard to concentrate on because all he was really thinking about and waiting for was the chance to take Storm walking.

He'd always give him a good brush first. He did that every day, as he'd been taught by Mr. Bouten. Not that it helped for long. The moment Flip finished, Storm would have a roll to get his coat back the way *he* liked it. And then they'd set off.

Flip's favorite spot was the north shore, the one closest to the farm. To get there, they had to walk through the sand dunes that ran the length of the island, protecting it from the sea. Capped with thick, bristly clumps of grass, they towered over both boy and horse and enveloped them in silence. As if sensing how small they made even *him* look, Storm would always walk closer to Flip in the dunes, pressing his flank against the boy's shoulder, so close Flip could feel the warmth radiating from his coat.

Then they'd step out onto the beach, where the sky stretched over their heads like some vast bright canopy and the wind raced over the waves into their faces. Storm's nostrils would twitch, as though the wind were tickling him. That always made Flip laugh, and when he did, Storm would turn to peer down at him before reaching down and nibbling at his pockets, looking for a piece of carrot.

After the first time that happened, Flip always made sure to take a handkerchief with him. A horse's nose, he'd learned, could make his pocket *wet.* And very, very sticky.

Storm liked the beach. He liked trotting along the sand or through the surf, though he never went far out into the water. Never more than up to his knees. Even then he wouldn't stay long. And not at all if Flip wasn't right beside him where he could see him. And feel him. He wouldn't ever go into the sea on his own.

From there they'd stroll on down to the lighthouse, several hundred yards away. It was a bright red pillar soaring up above the dunes at the eastern end of the island. Flip never forgot the first day he saw it, when low gray clouds clung to the island like mist, and its bright beam swept out through sheets of drifting rain to warn passing ships of danger.

As he'd stood staring up at the light, the only sound he could hear was the crash and hiss of waves on the shore and the wail of foghorns from invisible vessels out to sea. Then Storm had taken a single pace forward and rested his muzzle on Flip's shoulder. His breath had made little clouds of steam in the cold air and his mane had brushed lightly against the boy's cheek. For that brief moment, standing together on the sand, gazing up at the light cutting through the mist, it was as though he and Storm were the only two creatures alive in the whole world.

And that was wonderful. Just wonderful.

On most days, though, the sky was clear, and every time Flip reached the lighthouse, he'd stop at the base of the tower, gazing down over the island. He could see the beaches and the fields, the woods and roads and the village and the harbor. If it was low tide in the Wadden Sea, he'd stare at the endless stretches of sand and mud that glistened in the sun and attracted seabirds in the hundreds, hunting for worms and tiny sea creatures.

One day, he suddenly found himself wishing he could show his mom all this.

"She'd like it here," he said to Storm. "And we could show her the whole island, all the places we've been together. I really think she'd enjoy that."

Storm's ears twitched a little, then he stood still the way he always did when Flip mentioned his mother, as though he was paying extra attention.

With a start, Flip realized that it was the first time he'd thought about her in at least a week. Worse still, he realized that he couldn't picture her face clearly. When he thought of her, it was like looking at somebody through the bottom of a bottle. He could see her face but not her features. Her eyes and her nose and her smile—they were all beginning to fade. How could that have happened? He knew he'd been busy, with his work on the farm and with Storm, but how could he have forgotten what his mom looked like?

As much as he loved the island and as much as he loved Storm, how could he possibly have forgotten that?

19 ✳ *Heat*

FLIP WAS STILL thinking about this when he got up the next morning and went out to greet the horses. He was thinking about it so much that he forgot to lock the gate when he went inside for breakfast, and had to run back out and do so before Uncle Andries found out.

But he was just as forgetful after breakfast, which was probably the reason for what happened later.

It was a Saturday, and as soon as his chores were done, Flip returned to the field. Renske went with him. When they got there, they found the Ghost Girl sitting on the gate, feeding Storm and Leila pieces of an apple. She appeared every day now—although you could never tell when—and she always had something for the horses to eat. Sometimes she smiled. Sometimes she even laughed. But she still refused to speak.

To anyone.

The three of them sat on the gate and watched the horses. It was late summer and a hot, muggy day. The leaves hung limply from the trees, and the sky was a dull, hazy blue. Off in the distance, thunderclouds were piling up over the North Sea but, since there was no breeze to move them, they came no closer to the island.

Flip had brought a halter out to the field. But that morning he didn't feel like doing anything. He didn't want to walk around the field and he didn't want to walk along the beach. It was far too hot for that.

"Why don't you try riding him?" Renske suggested.

"I don't think he'll let me do that," Flip said.

"You haven't tried," said Renske.

That was true. He hadn't. He'd never ridden a horse in his life and the thought of doing it now, for the first time, scared him a little. Especially a horse as big as Storm. He'd always thought that was something for later, after he'd calmed him down. But what if he *could* do it now? What if learning to ride Storm was the key to getting him to accept the halter? That would be something to show Uncle Andries. And it would *really* impress his mom.

All his listlessness vanished in an instant. As soon as he could, he led Storm back to the gate by his mane and positioned him so that the horse's broad back was right next to it. Flip's heart was beating fast and he had butterflies in his stomach, but Storm didn't seem to notice and stood placidly beside the gate, letting Renske scratch behind his ears.

Taking a deep breath, Flip climbed the bars, took hold of the mane, and slid onto Storm's back. Or at least, he tried to. Because the moment he lifted his leg off the gate, Storm promptly took two steps sideways and Flip landed with a thump in the grass.

The Ghost Girl laughed. So did Renske. The ground was soft, so Flip didn't mind too much. But that morning, in the heat, the girls' laughter irritated him. He decided to try again. And to get it right this time.

He waited for Storm to return. When he did, he grabbed his mane and lifted his leg away from the gate. This time, Storm jumped backward and Flip landed with a crash on his stomach.

This happened again. And again. And again. Not once did Flip so much as manage to get seated on the horse, let alone ride him. After an hour he was covered in grass stains and stiff all over, but he wasn't about to give up. If anything, all his failures just made him more determined to succeed. And Storm didn't seem to mind him trying.

So back to the gate they went, where Storm blew out his breath and stood waiting patiently. Taking yet one more deep breath, Flip wrapped both hands in the mane and slipped smoothly onto the horse's back.

Storm didn't move a muscle.

Flip grinned. It had finally happened. Renske clapped her hands in delight and the Ghost Girl smiled.

"Give him a nudge with your heels," Renske said to Flip when Storm continued to stand still. "That tells him to move."

Flip did as she said and Storm took a step forward. Then a second, and then a third. Flip's grin was now almost as wide as his head. He couldn't believe he was actually riding! He gave Storm another little nudge and felt the horse break into a trot.

It lasted for six strides.

Storm, who obviously knew exactly what he was doing, stopped dead in his tracks and let Flip's momentum carry him forward. Flip flew through the air over the horse's shoulders and landed flat on his back in the mud beside the water trough. Over on the gate, Renske and the Ghost Girl were laughing again—Flip could see them trying not to, but having no success. As for Storm, he was all the way at the other end of the field, standing next to Leila and rubbing noses with her.

Right then, something snapped inside Flip. He was hot and sweaty, his head hurt from where he'd banged it falling down, and now he was covered from his face to his knees in clammy, clinging mud. He pulled himself upright and stood there in the baking sun, staring at the horses at the end of the field.

He'd been patient and kind. He'd never lost his temper. He'd done everything he could think of to help Storm adjust to his new surroundings. And what had happened? He'd just ended up thrown in the mud.

Storm had started back toward him again but Flip wasn't interested.

"You stupid horse!" he yelled at the top of his voice.

Startled, Storm galloped away.

Flip walked to the gate, flung it open, and strode off to the barn without a backward glance. He heard Renske saying something but he didn't pay her any attention. All he wanted to do right then was leave. He wanted his mother to come and get him and take him away from Mossum and never come back.

Ever.

Up in his room in the barn loft, he pulled off his muddy clothes and cleaned his face with a towel. Then he sat on the bed with his face in his hands and stared down at the floor. He could see the handle of the suitcase he'd carried all the way from Amsterdam peeking out from under the bed. At that moment it was more important than anything and he pulled it out and opened it to have a look, hoping it would cheer him up.

It didn't. It just made him feel worse, and before he knew it, tears flooded his eyes.

He didn't realize Aunt Elly was there until she spoke. The door wasn't shut and he hadn't heard her coming up the stairs.

"Whatever have you got *there*?" she said.

Flip sat up straight, wiping away the tears and hoping she hadn't noticed them.

"May I see?" She didn't sound angry. Just curious.

So he stepped aside to let her see what was inside the case.

20 * *The Suitcase*

It was a record player. A stereo record player. At first glance it looked like a big brown box, but when he unfastened the catches on the sides, it split into three parts. The bottom half was the turntable, with shiny black dials on the front and a thin silver spindle sticking up in the center. The top half was two boxes: the loudspeakers.

"Where did you get that?" Aunt Elly asked. Again, she wasn't annoyed. Just curious.

"It was Mom's," Flip said, trying not to sniff but not succeeding. "She bought it at the shop where she worked. A music shop."

"It looks terribly expensive," said Aunt Elly.

"It was," Flip said. "But what happened was, a man who bought it sold it back to the shop a month later because he needed the money. So because it was secondhand, Mom got to buy it much cheaper, and the owner of the shop let her because he knew how much his customers liked her. He said it was a sort of bonus. Otherwise she could never have afforded it."

Aunt Elly gazed admiringly at the record player. She touched the dials and picked up the speakers. "I've seen pictures of these in the paper. Stereo. Sound from *two* speakers. It's all terribly modern, isn't it?"

Flip nodded. "Mom was really proud of it. Nobody else we knew had one. The neighbors used to come around specially to listen to it. She was always playing her records on it. Until . . ."

He tried to finish the sentence but couldn't. Seeing the player hadn't made him feel better at all—only sadder.

"Until she left?" Aunt Elly suggested.

"Until she left," Flip agreed. Without thinking, he reached out and traced a cross with a circle around it on the turntable. "That's when I hid it."

"Hid it? From who?"

"Dad," Flip said. "He was so angry when she left he started smashing her things and I thought he was going to break that too. So I hid it."

"Didn't he know it was gone?"

"She'd put it in my room before she went, and he hadn't noticed. When he did see it was gone, I told him she'd taken it with her. And he believed me."

"And you've had it ever since?" Aunt Elly asked. "All this time?"

Flip nodded.

"None of us saw you bring it with you."

Flip felt embarrassed. He didn't know where to look. "That's because I hid it from Uncle Andries too."

Aunt Elly considered him with a kind but puzzled look in her eyes. "Why did you do that?" she asked.

Flip took a deep breath. "Because I heard him talking to our landlord when he came to Amsterdam," he explained. "The landlord said the rent hadn't been paid and Uncle Andries said *he* didn't have any money to pay it. So the landlord said he'd take all the furniture in our apartment as payment and Uncle Andries said that would be fine. So I hid the record player in my suitcase in case Uncle Andries found it and left it behind with everything else."

"Well, he certainly never noticed," Aunt Elly said. "And he wasn't the only one. How did you get it here?"

"In the suitcase," Flip said. "I carried it."

"All the way?" Aunt Elly said. "That can't have been easy. It must weigh a ton."

Flip thought of his aching fingers and battered knees on the walk to Amsterdam Central. "It does," he agreed.

"Very resourceful of you," his aunt said. Then she smiled again. "But your uncle wouldn't have sold it, you know. And besides," she added, pointing to one of his mom's singles that Flip had hidden and protected with the player, "he likes that Beatles song. He'd enjoy hearing that."

Flip was speechless. The idea that his uncle might actually like pop music—especially the Beatles—was too startling for words. He wasn't sure he could actually imagine his uncle liking *anything*.

Aunt Elly seemed to be able to read his thoughts. "He's not as bad as you think he is," she said. "Doesn't say much, I grant you. And he can look terribly forbidding at times. But if you'd told him about the record player, he'd have let you keep it. *And* bring it to the house to play it."

"Oh, it's not for me," Flip said. The words tumbled out of his mouth. "I don't want to use it. I didn't keep it for me. It's for Mom."

"For your mother?" Aunt Elly said.

"For when she comes back. It's a present. Just for her. I wanted to keep it perfect for *her*."

Again, Flip didn't know how Aunt Elly would react. But again, she surprised him.

"What a lovely idea," she said. "Good for you. After everything *you've* been through, I don't think many people would have thought to do that. You should be proud of yourself. And if you aren't proud of that," she went on, "then you should be for what you've done for Storm."

"Storm?"

"Yes," Aunt Elly said. "Storm. Renske told me what happened out in the field just now, and how annoyed you were."

Flip felt embarrassed all over again and started to apologize, but Aunt Elly shook her head.

"When I think of what Storm was like when he arrived and what he's like now, I can see you've done wonders," she said. "I know he's been annoying, but you've only been trying to ride him for an hour and that's hardly any time at all. You keep trying. That's what I came up here to say. You keep trying the way you have been. Because that's what makes *me* proud of *you*."

And with that, she walked back down the steps and across the yard into the farmhouse.

Flip watched her go, feeling all sorts of strange thoughts and emotions racing around inside his head. He thought about what Aunt Elly had just said, and about Storm and how much he'd grown to love exploring the island. It made him realize that life on Mossum wasn't turning out *at all* the way he'd expected.

But with a sinking heart, he realized something else. That even with the record player to look at, he still couldn't really remember his mom's face.

Then Renske burst into the room and he found out that he had an even bigger problem.

21 * Village in the Sand

"STORM'S GONE!" SHE gasped.

Her hair was a tangled mess, there was mud on her clothes, and her cheeks were wet with tears. The whole story spilled out of her before Flip could even ask one question.

"When Mama came up here to talk to you, the Mesman Boys went into the field. They said *they* could teach Storm to behave. They said *they* knew what to do. But he didn't like them, so he ran away from them and then they chased him until he ran right out of the field and I tried to stop him but he was too scared and he ran right past me and I fell over."

"Wasn't the gate locked?"

"No!"

Flip's whole body went cold as he realized he'd left the field without locking the gate. He'd forgotten to do the *one thing* that would at least have kept Storm where he belonged. And he'd forgotten because all he'd been thinking about was impressing Uncle Andries and his mom. He hadn't considered Storm; he'd only been thinking about himself.

"We have to get him back," he said, jumping up. "Did you see where he went?"

"Along the road. But he won't come to me."

"What about the Mesman Boys?"

"They ran off when Storm escaped." Her face crumpled and fresh tears filled her eyes. "I'm sorry, Flip," she sobbed. "It's all my fault."

"No, it isn't!" he said. "It's mine. *I* forgot to lock the gate. So if anyone's to blame, it's me. Now, do you want to help me get him back?"

Renske's tears stopped and her eyes brightened at the prospect of helping with the rescue. "Can I really?"

Flip nodded. "But you can't tell anyone else what's happened. If we're lucky, we can find him and bring him back before anyone knows he's gone."

Side by side they walked casually across the farmyard, careful not to run and attract attention. As he'd expected, the Ghost Girl was nowhere in sight. Nor were the Mesman Boys. Leila was standing just outside the open gate, eating grass at the roadside. They led her back into the field without a problem.

Storm wasn't nearly so easy.

He hadn't gone much farther down the road than Leila. But every time Flip and Renske got close enough to touch him, he trotted away out of reach, just the way he had the day he ran off to The Eyes. He didn't want to be caught and Flip didn't blame him: Flip had shouted at him and then failed to protect him from the Mesman Boys. Well, he'd have to protect him now, by getting him safely home, whatever it took. Without stopping to think about it, he ran back and snatched the rope and the halter from the gate and set off again in pursuit. Renske ran beside him.

They went past the Hofstra farm, past The Eyes and the camping ground behind the sand dunes on the north of the island. Storm was always in sight, but if they drew near, he just snorted, flicked his tail, and trotted away out of reach.

And that was how, after half an hour of running, stopping, and *almost* catching him, the two of them reached the beginning of The Yellow. And when they did that, they stopped and stared ahead of them with sinking hearts.

The Yellow was what the islanders called the long, flat, empty plain of sand that occupied almost the entire western third of the island. It stretched out as far as Flip and Renske could see, all the way to a dark blurred line on the horizon.

That line was all that was left of the village of Mossum. The *first* village of Mossum—not the one he'd ridden through when he'd arrived. He'd heard all about it on his second day on the island because Aunt Elly had sat him down and told him she didn't ever, *ever* want him going out there and the sooner he knew the reason why, the better.

The Wadden Islands hadn't always been the shape they were today, she said. The North Sea winds and currents were constantly pushing and pulling and stretching them out like bits of bubble gum, piling new sand up at one end, ripping and tearing it away at the other.

Two hundred years earlier, Mossum's first village had been a bustling little community surrounded by fields. But the wind and the sea had gradually pushed the sand right up to its edge and then over and around it. The villagers weren't there when that happened. They'd seen what was coming and long since departed to build a *second* village, the one Flip knew. They hadn't done anything about the old buildings, though. They'd just left them behind, to be reclaimed by the elements. All that remained now were a few crumbling walls and roof beams poking up out of the sand.

"And you are *never* to go out there," Aunt Elly had said, pointing a finger at him, with no trace whatsoever of her customary smile, "because the whole of The Yellow is covered in quicksand. There are pools of it everywhere, and they come and go because that's what quicksand does. It moves. It *drifts*. Which is why there isn't a map of it—because the pools are always shifting position. And if you step into one of them, there's no telling how long you'll stay in it. *If* you're lucky, someone'll see you and fetch help. If you're not, you'll stay stuck until the tide comes in and drowns you. And it comes in so fast you won't believe it. Or, if it's winter, you'll freeze to death first. Islanders don't *ever* go out there, and as long as you're an islander, you won't either. Do you understand?"

Flip nodded. And he never had. Now, he knew, he was going to have to break that promise.

It was hotter than ever and the sun was burning down on their bare heads from a clear blue sky. But when he looked away to his right and the distant North Sea, he could see the same clouds he'd seen earlier, darker now and higher and wider. A weak gust of warm air brought the faint hiss of waves breaking on the shore to his ears.

And down below him was Storm, ambling off across

the barren sands toward the vague blurred shape of the vanished village in the distance. Flip was afraid that at any moment the horse would step into a pool of quicksand and get stuck. But that didn't happen. Storm wandered a long looping path that never ran straight for more than a few feet. It was as though he could sense where the quicksand lay and was sticking to solid ground, no matter what direction it took him in.

"What are we going to do?" Renske said.

"We're going to go and get him," Flip said.

Renske's face paled. "Out *there*?"

Flip knew exactly how she felt. The thought of walking out into The Yellow made him nervous too. Actually, it terrified him. "We've got no choice," he replied. "We can't leave him. What if he gets stuck? We *have* to go and get him *back*."

Renske nodded. The breeze blew her hair back and forth across her face. "But I'm frightened," she said.

"You don't have to come. You can stay here."

"That'd frighten me even more. Standing here watching you."

"Then we'll go together," Flip said. "And we'll only walk where Storm's walked. If the sand supports him, it'll easily support us."

Renske looked doubtful. "Do you promise?"

Flip nodded. "I promise."

"All right," she said. "But you have to hold my hand." When he hesitated, she added, "I promise I won't ever tell anyone you did."

He smiled and took her hand.

Together they set off down the slope. But they hadn't gone more than a few paces when they heard footsteps behind them and turned to see the Ghost Girl darting down the side of the dune. She ran straight past them and stopped in Storm's tracks, staring off at the faint figure of the horse in the distance.

"*You* can't come!" Flip said.

She ignored him and started walking.

"I mean it," he repeated, letting go of Renske and running after her. "You can't! It's dangerous!"

All the Ghost Girl did was walk faster.

"All right," he said, realizing that the longer he stood and argued, the less time they had to get Storm back, "you *can* come. But only walk where Storm's walked. That way you know it's not quicksand."

The Ghost Girl rolled her eyes and nodded impatiently, as if to say she knew all that and why didn't they just get *going*!

So Flip took Renske's hand again and the three children set off across the empty plain. The only sound was the pad of their footsteps on the sand and, from far ahead, the soft thump of Storm's hooves. Every so often he would stop and sniff the air and the ground in front of him, then change direction. He never looked back or paid any attention to their calls to stop. Flip began to wonder if the horse was testing him, to find out how far he'd go and what he'd risk to get him back. Whether that was true or not, Flip realized he'd do anything to save Storm—anything to keep him safe.

And he kept walking.

He didn't realize how far they'd come until he turned around and saw that the dunes where the Ghost Girl had joined them were little more than a blur on the horizon. When he turned back, it was to see Storm disappear behind a mound of collapsed bricks.

They'd reached the remains of the village.

There wasn't much to see. A few walls were still standing, poking up out of the ground like big cracked teeth. Beams of rotten wood, turned gray by the sun and the wind and the rain, lay in a tangled heap at the end of what had once been a street. A pile of splintered roof tiles creaked and snapped when he put his foot on it. And everywhere, all around them, were thick drifts of sand piled up against any surface that would stop them. It looked like yellow water lapping silently over the village remains.

They were all alone in a deserted village in the middle of a silent, empty landscape.

22 * Riders

At last, Storm had stopped. He stood still behind one of the crumbling walls, watching the three children. The breeze ruffled his mane.

"Now what are we going to do?" Flip asked.

"What do you mean?" asked Renske.

Flip pointed at the wall and the piles of tumbled brick and wood on either side of it. "We've got to go over that to get him. Whichever way we go, he'll probably just run off in the opposite direction."

"If we had something for him to eat, he'd stand still," Renske said.

Flip looked at their surroundings. "There's nothing here *to* eat."

That was when the Ghost Girl stepped forward. With a shy little smile, she tugged two stubby carrots from her pocket. She handed them to Flip, who edged closer to Storm and held them out carefully on the palm of his hand. Just as carefully, Storm leaned down and began to eat.

Breathing a sigh of relief, Flip lifted his other hand to take hold of his mane. But in all the excitement, he'd completely forgotten that he was carrying the halter.

The moment Storm saw it he backed away. His hoof crashed down on a roof tile, which flew into the air in splinters. Flip covered his eyes. Renske dived behind him. The Ghost Girl ducked sideways, stumbled on a chunk of wood, and fell against the bricks Storm had been standing behind. They shivered and creaked. Then, with a groan like a rusty window creaking open, they collapsed in a cloud of dust and chips of broken masonry.

This was all too much for Storm. He spun around and galloped away to safety. He stopped twenty paces off, twitching his tail from side to side and snorting with fear.

Only then did Flip notice the Ghost Girl.

She was lying on her side with her right leg buried beneath a section of the collapsed wall. Even though there were tears in her eyes, she still hadn't made a sound.

Flip knelt next to her and started tossing bricks aside. Renske helped him. When they were finished, all three of them stared down at the Ghost Girl's ankle.

It was red and swollen. Together, they helped her to stand up, only to watch her take one step and fall straight down again.

A sudden gust of wind, much stronger this time, made Flip look around. The sky behind them to the north had now grown even darker. He could see gray bands of rain falling far out to sea. That didn't worry him. What worried him was that the tide was coming in, and coming in quicker than he'd thought possible, just the way Aunt Elly had said it would. When they'd started out onto The Yellow, the sea had been out of sight. Now he could see the wind blowing spray off the tops of the advancing waves.

"We've got to go," he said.

"But she can't walk," Renske said. She'd seen the approaching sea too, and her eyes were wide with fright. Despite the heat, her teeth were chattering.

"Then I'll help her," Flip said.

"And Storm?" Renske said.

Flip looked over at the horse, still standing off at a distance, watching them carefully.

"We haven't got time to catch him. We have to get away! He'll just have to follow us."

"But what if he doesn't?" she said.

Flip shook his head and didn't answer. The thought of what might happen to Storm was too horrible to contemplate. But the two girls were his first responsibility. He had to make sure *they* were safe. So he bent down, helped the Ghost Girl to her feet, and put his arm around her waist. She hopped forward for three paces before losing her balance and collapsing in the sand. Flip landed on top of her.

They tried again and went another four paces before she fell. Flip decided to carry her piggyback. She wasn't heavy and it worked for a while. But by then, after all their walking and running to catch Storm, Flip was tired. Very tired. So it wasn't long before *he* stumbled and fell. As he got to his knees and glanced back, he saw that the incoming tide had already swallowed up all trace of the deserted village. Waves were lapping at the path they'd taken just over one hundred yards away. A cold lump of fear grew in his stomach as he realized that they wouldn't get off The Yellow before the sea engulfed them. One glance at Renske and the Ghost Girl told him they were as scared as he was.

A sound at his back made him turn. Storm was standing over him, staring down into his face. This time, when Flip stood up and reached out to him, the horse didn't run away. He came closer and let Flip wrap both hands in his mane. Then he lowered his muzzle until it rested against the boy's forehead.

"You came to help us," Flip whispered, "didn't you?"

He lifted his head and gazed deep into Storm's eyes. Storm gazed calmly back. His breathing was slow and steady and wonderfully reassuring.

"But if you *do* help," Flip said, "then you're going to have to do something you don't like."

Storm peered patiently down at him, as if he could understand every word being spoken. Flip could see the two girls giving him funny looks but he didn't feel silly. He'd grown so used to talking to Storm by now that it felt totally normal.

"You have to let someone ride on you," Flip said. "And it's not me. It's the two girls."

"He won't do *that*!" Renske protested.

"Yes, he *will*," Flip said. "Because I've asked him."

Very slowly, he led Storm over to the Ghost Girl, reached down, and helped her to her feet. He told her to lean against Storm, then cupped her good foot in his hand, took a deep breath, and heaved her up into the air.

Storm's head twitched as she landed on his back. He took a step forward and then a step backward. He swung his head around to glance at the Ghost Girl.

And then he stood perfectly still.

"That's good, Storm," Flip said. "That's just what we need. I knew you could do it."

Then he turned to Renske. “Now you,” he said.

In one smooth movement, up she went. Storm took another step forward and backward when she landed on his back, but he didn’t try to shake her off. Or run away.

“And now there’s just one last thing,” Flip said, stroking the horse’s muzzle. “I have to put the halter on you.” He saw Renske staring but there wasn’t time to explain. “I really have to do this, Storm,” he said, unfastening the buckle and lifting it up. “So the girls can hold on to your mane and I can hold on to the rope.”

Storm didn’t like it. He said so with a lot of snorts and ear-twitching. But as if he could sense the need for it, he let the halter slide up over his muzzle and the strap go over his head behind his ears. Without being asked, the Ghost Girl leaned forward and fastened the buckle.

Flip attached the rope to the halter and with a gentle tug they were off, trotting back across the sand along their original path. Because their journey out to the village had never been in a straight line, they sometimes had to travel in the opposite direction to the dunes, and when they did, it meant walking back into the incoming tide. The waves rushed and gurgled around their ankles and that was when Flip was most frightened. He couldn’t see where he was stepping. All he could do was hope that Storm could still sense where the quicksand was and avoid it, just as he'd avoided it on the way out to the village.

Out of the water they went and then back in, sometimes for just a few paces, at others for whole minutes. Up on Storm's back, Renske clung to the Ghost Girl and the Ghost Girl clung grimly to Storm's mane. The two of them bobbed around like socks on a clothesline. Flip could see the fear in their eyes, but there was no time to stop and reassure them. As a wave surged around his ankles yet again, he urged Storm into a trot. The sand dunes were coming ever closer, but there was a long way still to go.

And then the very thing he'd been scared of since setting off happened. His left foot plunged down into the sand under an incoming wave and kept going. Before he could stop himself, both feet were sinking.

Into a pool of quicksand.

He held on to the rope. But only barely. Storm stopped trotting when Flip couldn't move but the horse's forward motion almost pulled the rope from his hands. His palms burned as it tore through them. Wincing with pain, he wrapped it around his wrists and held tight. Beneath him, the quicksand was still giving way under his feet, pulling him down farther and farther. His knees were now below the incoming waves and still he was moving downward.

"Go, Storm," he yelled. "Go!"

And Storm did. He put his head down, bent his legs, and moved off. The rope tightened and dug deep into Flip's skin. His arms felt as though they were being pulled from their sockets. But he stopped sinking. Stretching forward, he looped the rope once again around his wrists. By now he was almost horizontal to the sand and water.

Then, with a strange kind of wet *POP* he was free, sprawled full length on his front and being dragged through the surf. Urging Storm not to stop, he struggled to his knees, then to his feet, and stumbled on forward beside him. The dunes were dead ahead now and the incoming tide was at their backs. Before he knew it, they were up off The Yellow and on firm, safe ground.

Flip, completely exhausted, dropped to his knees and let the rope fall from his fingers. Up on Storm's back the girls were laughing out loud with relief. Storm, who wasn't even breathing hard, walked over to Flip and bent down to sniff at his face. Forcing himself upright on wobbly legs, Flip wrapped his arms around the horse's neck.

"Thank you," he whispered, pressing his face into the horse's side. "I *knew* you could do it. Thank you!"

Storm gently rubbed his nose on Flip's face, blowing warm air down his nostrils.

"And I'm sorry I shouted at you," Flip added. "You're not stupid at all."

Storm rubbed his nose harder, this time in Flip's hair, and Flip nearly fell over backward. The girls laughed at that, and this time, so did Flip. Right then, he really didn't mind a bit.

Finally, when he'd regained his strength, he took the rope in his hand and led everyone to the farm. Soon they were passing Leila's field. She ran over to the fence to say *hello* and followed them all the way along to the gate. Storm nickered a *hello* back. That made the girls giggle.

But they stopped when they entered the yard and saw Aunt Elly standing beside the front door. Uncle Andries was standing beside her.

And neither of them was smiling.

23 * *Flip's Punishment*

Flip hadn't given a moment's thought to what he would tell his aunt and uncle. But as it turned out he didn't have to, because as soon as they entered the farmyard, Renske did all the talking for him.

"Storm escaped," she babbled. "He ran away when the Mesman Boys tried to ride him and we went after him, all the way to the dunes, and there he was, down on the sand, all by himself, and we had to rescue him because we couldn't leave him there all alone. I was scared, but Flip held my hand all the way to the village and I didn't have to worry hardly at all."

Aunt Elly was incredulous. "You went to the deserted village? You went out onto *The Yellow*?"

"It's where Storm went," Flip explained, feeling the grown-ups' eyes boring into him. "He wouldn't come back, so we had to follow him. We couldn't leave him there."

"And you took the *girls* with you?" Uncle Andries demanded, looking angrier by the second.

"We wouldn't let him go *without* us," Renske said proudly. "We like Storm as well. And you can't be angry with Flip, because he got Storm to let us ride on his back after the wall fell on the Ghost Girl and the tide started coming in. He rescued *us* too. He was really brave. *And* clever."

Because of the way Storm was standing, the Ghost Girl's injured ankle was facing away from everyone. As soon as Aunt Elly heard that she had been injured, she went to the Ghost Girl to take a look.

"Does it hurt?" she asked.

The Ghost Girl nodded.

"Come inside and let me have a look at it."

The Ghost Girl shook her head.

"I won't hurt you," Aunt Elly said. "I promise."

The Ghost Girl shook her head a second time and tightened her grip on Storm's mane. Uncle Andries walked over and held up his hand. "Can you push my fingers?" he asked her. "With your foot?"

This the Ghost Girl did. He moved his hand up and then down and asked her to repeat the action. She did, both times.

"She can move her ankle," he said. "So it's not broken. I think she should go home."

"She can't walk," Aunt Elly said.

"I know," he said. "But she can ride."

"On Storm?"

"Yes," he said, looking coldly determined. "On Storm. And Flip can take her. I'll go with them. That can be his punishment: explaining to this girl's mother what happened. *Renske's* punishment I'll leave up to you."

Without another word, he beckoned Flip to follow him and set off out of the yard.

24 * The Ghost Girl's Name

The Ghost Girl's home nestled in the dunes not far from the lighthouse. From a distance, with its thatched roof, redbrick walls, and V-shaped line of pine trees at its back, it looked small and cozy. But as they drew closer, Flip saw that the grass at the front was ragged and uncut, the windows were thick with grime, and a child's bicycle lay on its side by the front door, covered in mud.

It looked sad and deserted.

The front door swung open and a woman ran down the path toward them. Her hair was untidy, her eyes were red-rimmed, and her face was drawn. She looked sad and tired.

"*There* you are!" she said to the Ghost Girl. "Where have you *been*?"

Uncle Andries stepped forward. "Mrs. Elberg," he said, taking off his cap, "I'm Mr. Bor. Your daughter was with my nephew, Flip. She had an accident. We brought her here as quickly as we could."

"Accident?" said Mrs. Elberg. "What happened?"

"My nephew can tell you," Uncle Andries said.

"Some bricks fell on her," Flip said. "On her ankle. She couldn't walk. So I put her on the horse."

In an instant, the tiredness vanished from Mrs. Elberg's face. She stepped to Storm's side, took her daughter's injured ankle gently in her hands, and probed it with her fingers. Then she turned to Uncle Andries.

"Mr. Bor," she asked, "would you be kind enough to carry my daughter inside?"

Uncle Andries nodded and reached up. This time, the Ghost Girl didn't protest. She let herself slide off Storm's back and into his arms. Flip watched him take her into the house and upstairs. A little while later, his uncle returned.

"Right," he said, tying the rope of the halter to the gatepost and stepping back from the horse, "I'll stay here with Storm. You go in and tell Mrs. Elberg exactly what happened."

Flip hesitated.

"A man tells the truth, Flip," his uncle said, looking calm rather than angry. "Whether it hurts him or not, he tells the truth. Now, in you go."

Flip stepped into the house and walked down a dark and gloomy hallway to the living room. Inside, he saw a pile of unopened cardboard boxes in front of a window with the curtains drawn. Drifts of ash spilled from a cold fireplace. He turned around as Mrs. Elberg came into the room. She looked him up and down.

"Your clothes are wet," she said. "You must be cold." She went to a cupboard, took out a blanket, and wrapped it around his shoulders. Then she walked over to the sofa before the fireplace and sank down into it. She patted the cushion beside her. "Sit down," she said.

Flip did as he was told. His heart was thumping in his chest, even though she didn't look particularly angry.

"Your name's Flip, is that right?" she asked.

"Yes," he said. "Is your daughter all right?"

Mrs. Elberg nodded. "She's fine. It's only a twisted ankle. I bandaged it up. This time tomorrow, she'll probably be back to running around like the streak of lightning she normally is."

"Doesn't she need to go to the doctor?"

"My husband was a doctor," Mrs. Elberg said sadly. And the sadness seemed to surround her, to swamp her. "I helped him with a *lot* of twisted ankles. She'll be fine." She reached out to turn on a lamp beside her. "But now I'd like to know what happened."

Still nervous, Flip began to recount everything that had taken place. He kept expecting Mrs. Elberg to blow up at him any moment over what he'd done. But she didn't. She listened intently. And when he got to the part about the Ghost Girl following Storm out onto The Yellow, she even smiled, although that was sad too.

"That didn't bother my daughter," she said. "Did it?"

"I told her it was dangerous," Flip said. "She wouldn't listen."

"She never does," Mrs. Elberg said. "She never listens to *anybody.* Not even to me, her own mother."

Flip told her the rest of the story.

"And how is the horse?" Mrs. Elberg asked when he finished.

"He's fine," Flip said. "Actually," he continued, his nervousness suddenly forgotten as he realized how proud he was of Storm, "he's amazing. He saved us. All of us."

"What's his name?" Mrs. Elberg asked.

"Storm."

"He's the horse you rescued from the sea, isn't he? I heard about that in the village."

"We rescued him," Flip said.

Mrs. Elberg looked puzzled. "*We?*" she said. "You and Renske?"

"Me and your *daughter*," Flip said. "Didn't she tell you?"

All of a sudden, Mrs. Elberg looked sadder than Flip thought it was possible for anyone to look. A tear slid down her cheek.

"My daughter doesn't tell me anything, Flip. She hasn't said a word to me since the accident." Her voice was suddenly anguished, and Mrs. Elberg dabbed at her face with a handkerchief. "We live in The Hague," she explained softly. "That's where my husband was a doctor. One night he was in a hurry to get to a patient. It was dark and it was raining and he slipped trying to run across the road in front of a tram. He was killed instantly." She breathed in deeply, almost choking back a sob. "That was nine months ago. Sophie hasn't spoken a word since. Not to me. Not to anyone."

"Is that her name?" Flip asked. "Sophie?" He found it hard to think of the Ghost Girl having an ordinary name. As if she was an ordinary girl, not this mute creature who came and went like a little ghost.

Mrs. Elberg nodded. "So she doesn't talk to you, either?"

"She's never said a word to me. I call her—" Flip hesitated, not sure whether he should continue. But then he thought that Mrs. Elberg probably couldn't get any sadder. "I call her the Ghost Girl."

Mrs. Elberg sighed. "She *is* a ghost. That's what she's become. I never know where she is half the time and the other half she's so quiet it's as if she's not even in the same house. I thought if I brought her *here*, to Mossum, away from The Hague and everything that reminds her of her father, she might cheer up. I thought she might start to talk again."

She rubbed her eyes.

"But it hasn't helped. It hasn't done anything, which is a great disappointment. She's *still* a ghost. We're leaving soon and she'll probably still be a ghost when we do."

She lapsed into silence and stared into the ash-filled fireplace. Another tear ran down her cheek. She wiped it away and offered Flip a thin smile.

"You should go," she said. "There's your poor uncle standing outside while I'm in here moaning about my problems. He'll be wondering what's happening."

The two of them walked outside.

"I want to thank you, Flip, for looking after Sophie," Mrs. Elberg said when they reached the front gate. "And I want to thank you for bringing her back. I'm glad she's got a friend here, even if she never does say a word to you. I'm glad she met someone who was nice to her. It'll give her something good to remember when she gets home."

She turned around and went inside the house before Flip could reply. *I'm glad I met your daughter too*, he wanted to say. *I was lonely here and she rescued me from the Mesman Boys. And if it wasn't for her, Storm wouldn't be here at all.* But Mrs. Elberg was gone.

Uncle Andries looked down at him. "Did you tell her what happened?" he asked.

"Yes," Flip said. "I told her."

"Everything?"

"Yes. Everything."

"What did she do?"

Flip tried to think of the most honest answer. "She just got sad," he said at last. "Because her daughter never talks to her. She wasn't angry with me."

Uncle Andries thought this over and gave a brief nod. Motioning Flip to untie Storm, he set off back toward the farm. Neither of them spoke. The only sound was the thump of Storm's big hooves on the sandy road.

Eventually, Flip knew he had to speak. Taking a deep breath, he said, "There's something I didn't tell you."

Uncle Andries stopped and stared down at him, waiting.

"I didn't lock the gate after me," Flip admitted. "*That's* the reason Storm got out. Not the Mesman

Boys, like Renske said. They just upset him. If I'd locked the gate like I should have, they couldn't have left it open when they came in and he'd never have escaped. It was *my* fault."

Uncle Andries shook his head.

"Well, you should have locked the gate," he agreed. "But it was the Mesman Boys scared him off. You shouldn't feel bad about anything those little hooligans do. Ever. I'm glad you told me, though. Good for you."

Flip nodded. But he could tell from Uncle Andries's face that there was something else he wanted to say.

"Are you still angry with me?" he asked.

Uncle Andries shook his head. "No," he said. He paused. "It's just that I've got some bad news. About Storm."

Flip stopped dead in the middle of the road. When he spoke he could hardly get the words out of his mouth. "Is something going to happen to him?"

"Yes," Uncle Andries said. "We're going to have to find him another home."

25 * No Money

"WHY?" FLIP DEMANDED. "I thought you said you weren't angry. And you agreed it wasn't his fault he escaped—"

Uncle Andries cut him off. "It's because we can't afford to keep him." He walked on for a few paces before continuing. "Your aunt and I have known it for a day or two now and we were planning to tell you this evening. Him running out onto The Yellow has nothing to do with it at all."

"But he's out in the field," Flip said. "All he's eating is grass! You don't have to pay for grass!"

"No, you don't," Uncle Andries agreed. "But that's in the summer, and the summer's coming to an end. And you can't keep a horse outside in winter. It's far too cold, which means he'll have to come inside. If he comes inside, he has to have hay and feed. Not to mention shoes if he's going to work. *That's* what we can't afford."

"It can't be that much," Flip said. "Just food for one horse."

Uncle Andries stopped and looked down at him. "Do you know that tin on the top shelf in the kitchen?" he asked.

"The cocoa tin?" Flip said. "Next to the cookie jar?"

Uncle Andries nodded. "That's where your aunt keeps our housekeeping money. Do you know how much is in it?"

"No," Flip said.

"Well, I do," Uncle Andries said, "because I counted it up at lunchtime. Three hundred and sixty guilders. And that's *all* we've got until the end of the month, to buy food for all of us. Not to mention a new coat for Renske before she goes back to school in the autumn. And you'll probably need something too. Three and sixty guilders won't buy all that *and* extra feed for an extra horse. And there's not going to be much more than that in the months to come."

He was silent for a moment.

"I'm sorry, Flip," he continued. "You rescued Storm and looked after him and made a friend of him. And you've taught him a lot. You've really persevered, so we know what he means to you. But we can't afford to keep him. It's as simple as that."

He turned away and set off slowly back toward the farm. Flip watched him go, then all of a sudden rushed to catch up. An idea had just occurred to him.

"What if you *did* have enough money," he said. "Could Storm stay then?"

"Flip," Uncle Andries said patiently, "we *haven't.*"

"Yes," he said, "but *if* you did, could he stay?"

Uncle Andries looked as if he really didn't want to talk about Storm anymore. Even so, he nodded his head and said, "If by some strange miracle, there was enough money to pay for him, then yes, I suppose he could. But since there isn't, he can't, and there's no more to be said on the matter. There'll be no more discussion."

Flip nodded and remained silent the rest of the way to the farm. He took Storm into the barn, rubbed him down, and gave him a good brush and some food, then put him back in his field. He hung up the halter and went inside for supper. He didn't say a word during the entire meal. As soon as he was finished, he asked to leave the table.

"I'm really tired," he said. "I'd like to go to bed."

"Oh, Flip," Aunt Elly said, misunderstanding what he was thinking. "Try not to be angry. You know we don't *want* to say good-bye to Storm."

Flip stopped at the door and turned to look at her. "I'm not angry," he said. "Really, I'm not."

And he wasn't. He wasn't angry, because he knew how he could find the money they needed to keep Storm on the farm. He raced off to the barn to make plans.

26 * *Cheated*

THE NEXT DAY, Flip did all he could to hide his intentions. He said little and walked around with a long face while he did his morning chores. When he'd finished, he asked if he could be excused and go into the village.

When Aunt Elly said yes, he ran to his room and took the suitcase from under his bed. On top of it went a piece of cardboard he'd found on a shelf in the barn, together with a wax crayon he'd borrowed from Renske. He carried them all to the center of Mossum and sat down on the grass in front of the church tower.

From the suitcase, he took out the record player. He opened it up so passersby could clearly see the loudspeakers and the turntable. Then he wrote FOR SALE on the piece of cardboard with the crayon and under that 3 YEARS OLD. *HARDLY EVER USED.* ONLY 200

GUILDERS. He placed the piece of cardboard on the grass in front of the record player and waited.

It didn't seem wrong to sell the player now. At least, not to Flip. Even though he'd kept it just for her—*protected* it for her—if everything went the way he hoped, he'd have something far *better* to show her when she arrived on Mossum. He'd have a horse. A horse he'd rescued and looked after, and who *listened* to him. He felt sure she'd appreciate that far more than any record player, however nice or expensive it was, especially since she liked horses so much herself.

A voice dragged him out of his thoughts. "Isn't that a lot of money to ask?"

He looked up to see a man and a woman staring down at him.

Flip reached into his pocket and pulled out the receipt for the player. His mom had kept it. She'd always kept receipts and now Flip was ever so glad she had, because not only did it prove how old the player was but also how much it had cost.

"My mom bought it when it was only a month old," Flip said, holding the receipt up, "for four hundred guilders. And then she only used it for two months. The rest of the time it's been sitting in a case all locked up, so it's practically brand-new. There isn't a scratch on it anywhere."

The couple agreed that it was in excellent condition, but even so, they shook their heads. "Still too much for us," they said, and walked away.

Flip thought two hundred guilders for a record player that had hardly ever been used was an excellent price. He thought somebody was bound to snap it up in a matter of minutes.

He was wrong.

Plenty of people stopped to look at it. A lot of them asked Flip why he was selling it. He told them the truth, and most of them smiled at that and wished him luck before walking on. Others said they'd come on vacation to get *away* from buying things. And a few people said it looked like a good deal, but since they had suitcases and tents and rucksacks to carry back home, they wouldn't be able to take a record player as well. No matter *how* much of a bargain it was.

He sat on the grass and waited for an hour, his disappointment steadily growing.

And then another hour.

By that time the sun had moved around in the sky and was shining straight down on him. It got so strong he had to hold the FOR SALE sign up against his head to protect his eyes against the glare. Two teenage boys walking by said it looked like he was trying to sell himself and laughed. The girls they were with laughed even louder. Flip moved the sign down over his face to hide his embarrassment.

After he'd been there for three hours, Flip decided to give up. He felt ridiculous sitting on the grass, being stared at. It was obvious no one was interested in the record player and that it had been a bad idea all along to think someone would buy it. How stupid could he have been to think they would? But just as he was about to get up and leave, a voice cut into his thoughts.

"You there! What are you doing?"

Flip looked up to see Mr. Mesman staring down at him. He had his hands in his pockets and a big fat cigar protruding from his lips.

"I'm trying to sell my record player," Flip said, glancing away. He didn't want the hotel owner to see how dejected he felt.

"Then you should say so!" Mr. Mesman replied, still not bothering to take the cigar out of his mouth. "You won't get far in this world if you just hold up a sign and keep your mouth shut. Why are you selling it?"

Flip remembered how Mr. Mesman had tried to take control of Storm the day he'd been rescued and how angry the man had been when Uncle Andries had stopped him. He didn't think it would be a good idea to mention the horse, so all he said was "I just need the money for something."

"We all need *money*," Mr. Mesman said. "*Money* makes the world go around." He breathed out a big messy cloud of cigar smoke. "Well, I'll buy it. The hotel could use a good record player. Bring it inside."

Flip couldn't believe his ears. Here he'd been just about to pack up and go home and now someone wanted to buy it. He was so surprised he didn't move.

"Come on, come on, come on!" Mr. Mesman barked. "Before I change my mind. I haven't got all day, you know."

Flip packed the player into the suitcase and followed him into the hotel. They went into a small office behind the reception desk. Mr. Mesman pointed at a table. "Put it down there," he said. Then he stuck his head out of the office door. "Jan!" he called out. "Petrus! Thijs! Get down here! Now!"

When there was no reply, he leaned on the reception desk.

"I said *now*!" he bellowed.

Footsteps clattered on the stairs. A few seconds later, the three brothers crowded into the office. They stared at Flip with ill-disguised dislike.

"Now, *this* boy," Mr. Mesman said, pointing at Flip, "wants to sell his record player. He's been sitting outside in the sun for the past three hours trying to make some money while all you lot've been doing is *playing*.

Well, I'm going to buy it from him and I want you to pay attention and learn something. Understood?"

The three boys nodded like puppies.

Mr. Mesman bent over and examined the player carefully. He twiddled the dials on the front, pressed his fingers against the turntable, and picked up the arm and looked at the needle.

"Very good," he said. "Very good. I know this machine, you know. I've seen it before in the shops. Cost four hundred and seventy-five guilders if I'm not mistaken." He turned to look at his sons. "A businessman should always know the price of everything," he told them. Then he turned to Flip. "Where did you get it?"

Flip told him how his mom had bought it and showed him the receipt.

"The receipt," Mr. Mesman said. He read it through, folded it up, and stuck it in his pocket. "Clever of you to keep it. Well done. Smart lad." Producing his wallet, he counted out a sheaf of banknotes and handed them to Flip with a flourish. "And that, I think you'll find," he said, "is a *very* good deal."

Flip's excitement lasted only as long as it took to count the money.

One hundred guilders.

Mr. Mesman saw the disappointment on his face and asked, "Were you expecting more?"

"Yes," Flip said.

"*Really?*" Mr. Mesman asked, as if there couldn't possibly be any doubt about the price he'd offered. "How *much* were you expecting?"

"Two hundred guilders," Flip said.

Mr. Mesman stared down at him in silence. Then he smiled a smile that wasn't friendly at all. "But you said your mother bought it *secondhand*," he said. "And when you buy something secondhand, the price drops."

Flip could see the Mesman Boys out of the corner of his eye, smirking at him.

"But she hardly used it!" he protested. "And the person before her had it less than a month."

Mr. Mesman shook his head. "Doesn't matter," he said. "If it was *secondhand* when your mother bought it, that makes it *thirdhand* now. You don't expect me to pay two hundred guilders for something that's *third-hand*, do you? Why do you think nobody else bought it? All those people who stopped to look at it and then walked away? They were thinking exactly the same thing."

Flip started to say they weren't because they'd told him their reasons, but Mr. Mesman cut him off.

"I'm offering you a good price for what this record player is worth today, here on this island. After you've been out in the sun for almost three hours and *nobody's* shown the slightest interest in buying it. If you try selling it again tomorrow, I won't be so generous as I am now. And that's a promise."

Flip knew what was happening was wrong. But he didn't know how to convince Mr. Mesman. And he had to find a way to keep Storm. Keeping Storm was more important than anything else.

"I'll take the money," he said with a sinking heart as the three brothers looked admiringly at their clever father.

Flip left the hotel and stood on the steps with the money in one hand, the cardboard sign in the other, and an empty suitcase at his feet. From feeling ridiculous and stupid just a few minutes before, he now felt angry and humiliated.

"And that," he heard Mr. Mesman say to his sons inside, "is how you buy something for the price *you* want to pay. Not what the other person wants. Go on the attack and *stay* on the attack. Don't give them the chance to think straight. Do you idiots understand? Were you paying *attention* for once?"

Flip walked slowly home. When he got there, Aunt Elly was sitting outside in the afternoon sunshine with Renske. They were drinking glasses of lemonade.

"Ah, there you are!" Aunt Elly said. "We were wondering where you'd got to." Then she saw the look on his face. "What on earth's happened?"

Flip didn't answer. He didn't know what to say. He'd been such a fool.

"Have you stolen something?" she asked.

Flip shook his head.

"Have you murdered someone?"

"No!" Flip said. "Of course not!"

"Well, that's a relief," Aunt Elly said. "At least we know we're not living with a thief or a murderer. We won't have to lock our doors at night."

Renske giggled, which made Flip smile. Just a little. So he told Aunt Elly what had happened. When he was finished, she looked deep into his eyes.

"You sold the record player so Storm could stay here?" she asked.

Flip nodded. "I know I was keeping it for Mom, but I *couldn't* let Storm go! Not now! Not after everything that's happened. And I thought Mom would understand, because she likes horses too."

"Yes," Aunt Elly said. "I'm sure she would."

"But it's no good now," Flip said, feeling miserable, "because I didn't get enough money. I was hoping I'd make so much Storm could stay here for years and years! And then you'd never have to worry about feeding him again. He could stay here for the rest of his life."

Aunt Elly leaned forward and took his hand in hers. "*Fool me once, shame on you,*" she said. "*Fool me twice, shame on me.* Do you know what that means?"

Flip shook his head.

"It means," Aunt Elly said, "that if someone makes a fool of you once, it's not your fault. It's theirs, because they did it on purpose. But," and she held up a finger, "if they do it again, then it *is* your fault for not learning your lesson and stopping them. Now, this Mr. Mesman got your record player off you for less than it's worth. That wasn't your fault. You were being honest. He wasn't. He made you look like a fool in front of his sons *and* he cheated you. The only person who's done something wrong today is him, and I don't want you blaming yourself for a second for anything he did! Is that quite clear?"

Flip nodded.

"Good!" Aunt Elly said. She stood up, took off her apron, and tidied her hair. "Then off we go."

"Where?" Flip and Renske asked simultaneously.

"To the hotel," Aunt Elly said. "To get the *rest* of the money Flip should have been paid."

And without another word, she strode off to the village.

27 * *The Handclap*

MR. MESMAN WAS standing behind the reception desk, talking to two hotel guests, when Aunt Elly walked in. He frowned when he saw her, then frowned even harder when he saw Flip and Renske at her back.

"I want to talk to you," Aunt Elly said without raising her voice. "I'll let you finish your business with these two gentlemen, then I shall expect your full attention. Is that clear?"

Mr. Mesman was so surprised, all he could do was nod. Aunt Elly took the children and stood off to one side. When the guests left, she walked up to the desk.

"And what can I do for—" Mr. Mesman began.

"I'd like the rest of the money you should have paid Flip for his record player," Aunt Elly said, still speaking softly. "I'd like it now, I'd like it in cash, and I won't leave until I get it."

Mr. Mesman tried a smile. “Your nephew sold me his record player. If there’s a problem with the price he got, perhaps *he* should talk to me about it.”

“No,” Aunt Elly said. “He’s not going to do that because you’d only bully and bamboozle him all over again and send him out of here with even less than you paid him the first time. You’re going to talk to *me* instead.”

Mr. Mesman’s smile vanished. “The boy,” he said, “was selling a *thirdhand* record player. I gave him a good price for something thirdhand.”

“Rubbish,” Aunt Elly said. “That record player is in excellent condition and the only person who would call it *thirdhand* is either a cheat or blind. Are you blind, Mr. Mesman?”

“No,” Mr. Mesman said through gritted teeth. “I am not.”

“Then you’re a cheat and you should be ashamed of yourself.”

“How dare you!” he hissed. “I resent that!”

“Of course you resent it,” Aunt Elly said. “Cheats always resent the truth. But you’re still going to talk to me. And you’re still going to pay Flip what you should have the first time.”

“I’m not prepared to offer one cent more!”

"You most certainly are," Aunt Elly said, "because I'm not leaving until you do. That's the second time I've said this. Do I have to say it a third time?"

Passing hotel guests could hear the conversation and were casting curious glances at the group at reception. A few lingered to hear what was going on.

Mr. Mesman smiled at them. "Perhaps," he suggested to Aunt Elly, "we could talk in the office?"

"We can settle the matter quite satisfactorily out here," she said.

Mr. Mesman glanced at the guests out of the corner of his eye, then raised his right hand in frustration. "I'll pay an extra twenty guilders," he said.

Aunt Elly reached out and slapped his hand lightly. He stared at her as though she'd just stepped out of a spaceship.

"What are you doing?" he demanded.

"I thought *you* were doing the handclap," she replied.

He looked even more puzzled.

"The handclap," she explained, "is the way we country people trade at the market. The seller starts by stating a price. If the buyer doesn't agree, he slaps the seller's hand. So the seller makes a new offer and slaps the buyer's hand. This goes on until they reach a price they agree on. Then they *shake* hands. You know, if you *are* going to live on Mossum, Mr. Mesman, you really should learn your neighbors' customs."

"I can't afford to waste time with all that nonsense," he fumed. "I'll give you one hundred and fifty. In total!"

Aunt Elly slapped his hand again. "Two hundred."

More people were now peering in through the hotel's front door to see what was going on. Mr. Mesman saw them too. "One hundred and seventy-five," he said.

Another handclap from Aunt Elly. "Two hundred," she repeated.

Mr. Mesman glared at her and breathed in through his nose. It took him a long, long time. Then he breathed out. That took him even longer. Aunt Elly stared back at him without moving a muscle. The crowd outside the doors had grown even larger.

"All *right*!" the hotel owner snapped, tugging out his wallet and counting the extra notes onto the desk. He handed them to Aunt Elly, who gave them to Flip.

"I don't suppose there'll be a handshake," she said, "but don't forget to say thank you, Flip."

"Thank you," Flip said.

Mr. Mesman ignored him. "I wonder," he said to Aunt Elly, "why you let the boy stand there and fight his battles for him. What kind of lesson is that?"

"A better one than making your sons stand in a line to watch while you cheat someone," Aunt Elly replied. She took Renske's hand and turned to go.

"You won't be here long, you know," Mr. Mesman called after her. "I'll have your farm. One way or another, I'll have it. And when I do, there won't be any stupid handclapping, I can promise you *that*!"

Aunt Elly ignored him and led the children outside.

"What did he mean by that?" Flip asked. "About the farm?"

For a moment, Aunt Elly's cheerfulness seemed to desert her. She looked tired. Then she pulled herself together and smiled.

"Well," she said, "if you were to buy us all an ice cream, I might be persuaded to tell you all about it. I think a rich man like you could afford three ice creams, don't you?"

Flip went into the shop and bought three ice creams. Then they sat down on the bench in front of the church to eat them.

And Aunt Elly told him what Mr. Mesman had meant.

28 * A Luxury Hotel

"Mr. Mesman," Aunt Elly said, "wants to build a new hotel."

"He's already *got* a hotel," Flip said.

"I know he has," Aunt Elly said. "But he wants to build a new one."

"Where?" Flip asked.

"On our farm."

Flip couldn't believe his ears. "But that's your *home*!"

"Oh, that's not going to stop Mr. Mesman," Aunt Elly said. "He's got big plans. He wants to buy our farm, knock it down, and put up a brand-new luxury hotel, twice as big as the one he has now. And then he wants the rest of our land to build a huge park and playground for the guests, one that goes all the way down to the beach. That way they'll be able to walk straight from the hotel to the sea."

Flip thought about that for a moment. "But he can't build anything if you don't sell the farm to him," he said.

"He can't. You're right. But we may *have* to sell," Aunt Elly said. "The world's changing. Farms on the Wadden Islands are disappearing because people on the mainland can do things much more cheaply than we can. You used to be able to get by just dealing with your neighbors. But not anymore. Now there's cars and trucks and roads everywhere and everything's moving so much faster. You can trade with anyone anywhere in the country now. Small farmers like your uncle can't keep up. They can't earn enough money to keep up."

"Why doesn't Uncle Andries do something else?"

"Because he's a farmer. That's what he loves to do. His family's lived on Mossum for more than a hundred years."

"But if you don't have enough money, wouldn't it be better to do something else?" Flip said.

Aunt Elly was quiet for a while. "You like Storm, don't you?" she said at last.

"Yes," Flip said.

"If he went away, you wouldn't be happy, would you?"

"No."

"So when you found out he might have to go," she went on, "you did everything you could to keep him.

You didn't just say, *Oh well, I haven't got enough money, so I'll let him pop off and live somewhere else*, did you?"

"I couldn't do that!" Flip said. "Not to Storm!"

"That's the way your uncle feels about the farm," Aunt Elly said. "He's not going to give it up just because he doesn't have a lot of money. He's going to do everything he can to keep it. Just the way *you* did everything you could to keep Storm. The only trouble is, if anything bad ever happens and we suddenly need to pay a big bill, we won't be able to. *That's* what Mr. Mesman meant. He's hoping that one day, someday, your uncle's going to need more money than he's got. He's hoping your uncle will be forced to sell the farm, and then he'll jump in and snap it up before anyone else can make an offer."

"That's not fair!" Flip exclaimed.

"I know it's not," Aunt Elly said. "If things were fair, Mr. Mesman would look after the hotel he already owns. Or spend some money to help fix this church tower behind us. That big gap at the top's only going to get bigger, you know, and one day there'll be an accident. But Mr. Mesman isn't interested in the church. Or the island. All he wants to do is build his big new hotel and make a lot of money from it."

"I thought he *was* an islander," Flip said. "His sons call me *city boy*. I thought they'd always lived here."

"Rubbish!" Aunt Elly said. "They're city boys too. They've only been on Mossum four years. They came from Rotterdam."

"Then why do they call me—"

"*City boy?* Because bullies will use any excuse to pick a fight. If you'd been born on Mossum, they'd call you *a stupid islander.*" She held up her hand. "And that's the last breath I'm wasting on the Mesmans on a lovely afternoon like this. I'm not talking about them anymore. Now you know the story. That's enough."

The three of them fell silent and concentrated on eating their ice creams.

"I've always liked sitting on this bench," Aunt Elly said after a while. "Did you know your father helped put it here?"

"My dad?" Flip said. He was almost too surprised to speak. He'd never seen his dad make anything in his entire life. As far as Flip knew, all he'd ever done was stay out at night and come back home with a new stack of stolen boxes.

"Him and your uncle. When they weren't much older than you are now, they dug the holes and poured the concrete and set the legs in it. And then they painted it. I always think of your father when I sit here."

"Is this where he met my mom?" Flip asked. "On Mossum?"

"Yes," Aunt Elly said. "She came to work in the hotel for the summer. Then she went back to Amsterdam with your father."

"Did you know her?" Flip asked.

"Oh, only a little."

"What was she like?" he asked. "I mean, what was she like *then*?"

Aunt Elly considered the question. "Well," she said, "she was very pretty. *All* the boys were in love with her. And she liked the island. She liked to go walking and riding on it. In fact, I think she would have stayed on Mossum if she hadn't met your father. He was a handsome lad and all the girls were in love with *him*. Trouble was, he didn't want to stay."

"Why not?"

"It bored him."

Bored? Flip thought, amazed at this news. *How could anybody be bored on Mossum? How could you prefer a damp, poky little apartment in a noisy city when there was a whole island to explore?* He finished his ice cream and folded up the wrapper. He looked at Aunt Elly.

"I keep forgetting my mom's face," he said.

He felt bad saying it, as if he were doing something wrong. But Aunt Elly only smiled.

"Everyone does," she said. "If you haven't got a photo of someone and they aren't there every day, it's easy to forget what they look like. But it doesn't mean you've forgotten them."

Flip pulled the letter from his pocket. "I keep this, though. She wrote it to me before she left. It's worth even more to me than the record player."

He let Aunt Elly read it. When she had, she folded it up carefully and handed it back.

"You're a good person, Flip," she said. "And your mother would be very pleased about what you've done today. So will your uncle, when you tell him. In fact, I can't wait to see the look on his face when you do."

"It wasn't just me," Flip said. "You helped too."

"It was your idea to sell the record player," Aunt Elly said. "All *I* did was collect some outstanding cash. I hardly did a thing."

They left the bench and started walking home. Renske took her mother's hand and looked up at her with serious eyes.

"I'd have sold *my* record player too," she said. "If I'd had one."

Flip followed along happily behind them.

Bored? he thought. *How could you be* bored *on Mossum?*

29 * *Like a Magpie*

Flip waited until supper to give his uncle the money. He didn't know how to do it, or what to say, so after he'd helped clear the dishes away, he just took the notes out of his pocket and placed them on the table.

"This is for Storm," he said simply. "To pay for his food in the winter."

Uncle Andries stared at the money. "Where did you get this?" he asked.

Flip told him what he'd done, and how Aunt Elly had helped him.

Uncle Andries stared at him. He pushed the notes around on the table with his fingertip, as though he wasn't sure they were real. Then he looked at Flip. Then he looked at the money again. Then he stood up and walked out through the door into the farmyard without a word. He stayed away so long, Flip was convinced he'd done something wrong and he said so to his aunt.

"Not at all," she said, without pausing in the washing up. "I've never *seen* him so happy. He'll be back in a moment to shake your hand and he'll be chattering away like a magpie. Just you wait and see."

And a moment later, Uncle Andries *did* come back. He walked up to Flip, grabbed his hand, and shook it.

"Good lad," he said. There was a long pause. He swallowed and coughed and looked embarrassed. "Good lad," he said again, before adding in a voice choked with emotion, "Thank you."

And with that he spun around and went back outside.

"See," Aunt Elly said. "Couldn't get a word in edgeways, could you? I thought he'd *never* stop talking." She turned away from the sink. "He is happy, Flip," she said. "He really is. He's not the sort of man to say it but he is, believe me. Now, go on out and see Storm. He should hear the good news too."

Flip didn't hesitate. As he ran out to the field and climbed up onto the gate, Storm came running to greet him. Flip wrapped his arms around his neck and buried his head in the horse's mane. Storm rubbed his muzzle happily up and down against the boy's back.

"We're all right now," Flip whispered, pulling his head back and looking deep in Storm's eyes. Then he reached out, drew a little cross on the horse's muzzle with his fingertip, and enclosed it in a circle. "We're safe. You can stay. Everything's all right."

30 * *Revenge*

THE FOLLOWING MORNING, Flip found a cut on Storm's flank. He decided to clean it in the barn, after he'd brushed him and checked his hooves. Since it wouldn't take long, he didn't bother using a halter. He just wrapped his hand in Storm's mane and led him inside. When he was finished, he headed back out to the field, only to stop when he saw the Mesman Boys standing on the road in front of him, blocking the way.

"Well, well, well," said Thijs. "Look who it is."

"Got something *more* to sell?" Petrus asked.

"Going to get your *auntie* to help you?" Jan finished. "Make our dad look like a fool? In front of the guests?"

Of all the three, he seemed to be the angriest. His face was red and he looked as though he'd like nothing more than to knock Flip off his feet right then and there.

Flip remembered what Aunt Elly had said about how bullies looked for any excuse to start a fight and decided not to reply. But when he tried to walk Storm past the boys, Jan stepped in front of him.

"What's the matter?" he demanded. "Too good to answer? Think you're better than us, *city boy*?"

Flip guided Storm to the right and kept going. Jan stepped in front of him again and this time he pulled back his fist for a punch. The moment he raised his arm, Storm butted him in the stomach with his muzzle.

"*Ooof!*" said Jan, and he sat down hard in the middle of the road.

Thijs and Petrus came flying to his rescue but stopped in their tracks as Storm wheeled around on his back legs, pulling loose from Flip's grasp and crashing his front hooves down on the ground. The two brothers curled up in the road with their hands over their heads, quivering with fear.

Storm advanced on them again slowly, lowered his muzzle, and sniffed at their fingers. When he breathed out, the hair blew back off their foreheads and the two of them yelped like dogs.

Without a word, Flip wrapped his hand in Storm's mane and led him away. The moment the brothers realized they were safe, they scrambled to their feet and ran for the village.

Flip put Storm back in the field, but he didn't leave. He didn't think the Mesman Boys had gone for good and he wanted to be there if they returned. He sat down on the gate and waited.

Time passed. Nothing happened. There was no sign of the brothers.

Flip still didn't want to leave, but he was getting a little bored just watching the horses. So when Storm ambled up a little later to see if there was anything to eat, he decided to try something he'd been wanting to try again since that day on The Yellow. He reached out, wrapped his hands in the horse's mane, and slipped onto his back.

He was all ready to be thrown off again. But today Storm didn't seem to mind carrying Flip in the slightest. Not anymore. And when Flip gave him a little nudge with his heels, he turned and strolled gently away from the gate. He walked all the way up to the end of the field, turned, and walked back again. Leila trotted over to join them.

For Flip, it was magic. It was hard staying on—he couldn't believe how difficult it was to stay balanced—but just being up on Storm's back was more fun than he could ever have imagined. He'd never known anything like it in his life.

As they reached the far end of the field for the fifth

time and swung around, he saw the Ghost Girl appear by the gate. By now he was so happy, he'd forgotten why he was out in the field in the first place and he urged Storm forward to greet her. He knew she'd have an apple or a carrot hidden in a pocket and he thought Storm had more than earned it.

There was no wind. The sun shone down. The island was silent.

Halfway to the gate, Storm stopped.

His ears folded back on his head and he stood perfectly still, sniffing the air. A split second later, there was a buzz, followed by a snap as something smacked into his back, right beside his tail. He jumped as if he'd been given an electric shock.

Then came another buzz and another snap. Flip saw a pebble the size of his thumb bounce off Storm's shoulder. Head up, tail thrashing the air, Storm spun around only to stop dead in his tracks as a third pebble struck him in the side of the neck.

Clinging desperately to the horse's mane with both hands and squeezing tight with both legs so he wouldn't fall off, Flip swiveled his head in all directions, trying to see what was happening.

Standing in the shade of a tree halfway up the field, slingshot in hand, was Jan. In the trees to his left and his right were Thijs and Petrus. They'd formed a line across the field, cutting it in half.

All three let fly with their slingshots simultaneously. The pebbles zipped through the air, striking Storm on his left shoulder and right leg. An instant later, Jan fired a third pebble, straight at the horse's mouth.

Untouched by the stones, Leila had galloped away to safety. But Storm couldn't get away—the Mesman Boys wouldn't let him. Flip could see spots of blood welling up on the horse's neck and face where the pebbles struck him. Deathly afraid now, with head twitching and nostrils flaring, Storm tried desperately to escape the barrage, only to be struck wherever he turned. So he wheeled around and, with Flip slipping and sliding on his back, headed in the only direction left to him.

Toward the gate and the Ghost Girl.

Tossing his head and his tail as the pebbles continued to strike, he roared down the field with Flip clinging tight to his mane. The Ghost Girl saw them coming and threw herself backward.

And then, as another volley of pebbles lashed his flanks, Storm jumped.

It couldn't have lasted more than a few seconds, but to Flip those seconds passed like minutes. He felt the muscles in Storm's back and legs and shoulders bunch and heave. He heard the sudden silence as Storm's hooves left the ground and they flew through the air. And when he looked down he saw the Ghost Girl sprawled on her back in the grass, wide-eyed with fear and staring up at Storm's massive black body as it blotted out the sun and cast her into shadow.

With a thunderous crash, Storm landed on the far side, skidded in the soft ground, and righted himself. Flip couldn't hold on any longer. The mane flew out of his fingers and he sailed off sideways into the hedge. But Storm didn't stop. He didn't stop because the Mesman Boys were still coming, running down the field and firing as they ran. He kept going, using every scrap of strength and speed he possessed to escape the deadly rain of pebbles.

And he ran in the safest direction he could find.

Straight toward the village.

31 * Storm's Deadly Rampage

FLIP SCRAMBLED TO his feet and dashed after Storm. The Ghost Girl went with him. When they rounded the corner that led into the main street, a woman and two small children ran past them in the opposite direction.

"There's a wild horse!" the woman screamed, pointing behind her. *"A wild horse!"*

Flip sprinted on and reached the edge of the village just in time to see Storm gallop past the café. Vacationers scattered. Tables went flying. A chair rolled in front of him and was smashed to pieces under his hooves.

He headed toward the churchyard, but two men waved him away. That made him swerve to his right, knocking down a stack of plastic buckets and spades outside the gift shop and sending a rack of postcards fluttering into the air. A shout from the shopkeeper panicked him even more and sent him reeling back across the road into the boxes of fruit and vegetables stacked outside the grocer's. Apples, oranges, potatoes, and tomatoes sprayed in all directions.

Terrified by the constant yells and shouts of the people in the street, Storm tried to escape to the harbor. But a second group of men had seen him coming and had lined themselves up in the middle of the road with arms outstretched to cut off his escape. Rearing up with a whinny of fear that echoed off the buildings in the center of the village, he whirled around and headed back the way he'd come, skidding over the cobblestones.

The men who'd stopped him from entering the churchyard now appeared with a rope. They tried throwing it around his neck, but he ducked sideways, lurched to his left, and galloped along the side of the hotel.

But that way was blocked too. The road was filled by a cart carrying the luggage of the guests who'd just arrived on the afternoon ferry. Storm couldn't jump over it, or go around it, so he went in the only direction still open to him. With a bellow of fear, he galloped up the steps that led to the terrace at the back of the hotel.

And as long as he lived, Flip would never forget what happened next.

For a second or two, the guests lazing in the sun over a drink or a cup of coffee couldn't believe their eyes as Storm—eyes rolling and sweat now dripping down his flanks—thundered into view. Then they exploded into motion. Mothers seized babies. Fathers grabbed children. Screams rang out as chairs, tables, glasses, cups, and saucers crashed to the ground. The guests nearest the door to the hotel threw themselves through it. The guests on the far side of the terrace took one look at the snorting black shape roaring toward them and jumped, rolled, leapt, and sprang over the balcony rails like leaves swept away by a massive broom.

Behind them, frantically searching for an escape route, Storm lurched and lunged about in every direction. So closely packed together was the furniture on the terrace that his hooves couldn't help trampling everything they came in contact with. In seconds he was surrounded by splinters of wood, torn sun umbrellas, and broken glass and china. And with each new object he ran into, Storm became more and more terrified.

In desperation, he tried leaping over the terrace railing, but slipped on the wooden floor and smashed down onto his side as his hind legs went out from under him. In an instant he was back on his feet, but the shock of the fall had calmed him down, if only a little. He stood still, ears pinned back, breath rasping. A thin line of blood ran down one of his hind legs.

The men who'd tried to catch him before now ran up the steps and spread out in a new line at the entrance to the terrace. They advanced slowly, intent on tying him up, only to leap back when he spun around at their approach. He paced back and forth, his tail high in the air.

Flip tried to go to his rescue but was dragged back down to the street by grown-ups wanting to protect him. He tried telling people the horse was his and he knew what to do but nobody would listen. When he heard a man's voice talk about getting a gun, though, he knew it was time for something drastic.

He looked around, saw an apple on the ground in front of the grocer's shop, and snatched it up. Instead of trying to push his way through the people on the steps, he clambered up the outside of the banister. Just before he vaulted over the railing onto the terrace, he felt something fall from his pocket and looked down to see the letter from his mother flutter to the street.

Everything seemed to stop. Did he climb back down and rescue it? Or did he protect Storm? He knew he couldn't do both. There wasn't time. When he felt a hand reach out and clutch his shoulder to pull him back, his mind was made up. He leapt over the railing onto the terrace and strode forward before anyone could grab him again.

Storm was now so scared he didn't even seem to recognize Flip. When the boy approached, he backed up and stamped at the terrace with his forefeet. So Flip stopped, stood still, and waited. The watching crowd had fallen silent too, and the only sound to be heard was the horse's ragged breathing.

"This is for you, Storm," Flip said softly, crouching down on his haunches and holding up the apple on his open palm. "I brought it just for you."

Warily, Storm took a step forward. Flip didn't move a muscle. Storm advanced another step and lowered his head, sniffing at the apple. When he reached out to bite into the fruit, Flip straightened up as slowly as he could and gently took hold of his mane.

The moment he did so, the men at the top of the steps surged forward, only to be stopped in their tracks by two others who stepped in front of them.

It was Uncle Andries and Mr. Bouten.

"Leave the boy alone," Mr. Bouten said. "He knows what he's doing."

"If he knew what he was doing," someone called out, "he wouldn't have let that horse escape in the first place."

Other voices agreed. Soon everyone was talking all at once to anyone who'd listen about what had happened. And that was the moment when Flip saw the three Mesman Boys, lurking at the back of the crowd.

"They're the ones!" he called out. "They're the reason Storm escaped!"

All the talk on the terrace ceased.

"And how," demanded Uncle Andries, "did they do that?"

Flip told him everything he'd seen, but before he was even halfway through his story, the Mesman Boys were saying, "No, we didn't!" and "We were on the beach!" and "He's lying!"

"I'm *not* lying!" Flip said. "Ask Mrs. Elberg's daughter . . . Sophie. She saw them too."

But of the Ghost Girl there was, as ever, no sign at all. She'd vanished just as she always did.

"So," said a new voice, "it's your word against theirs. Is that right?"

It was Mr. Mesman. He walked up to his sons and put his hands on their shoulders. He didn't seem the slightest bit worried about what had just happened to his terrace. In fact, Flip was almost sure there was the ghost of a smile on his face.

"My sons say they were on the beach. You say they weren't. Are we expected to take your *one* word against their *three*? I don't think that's very fair."

Flip saw a few nods in the crowd.

"And that horse *has* escaped before," Mr. Mesman continued. "Every islander's heard about the trouble he's gotten himself into. All his little escapades. Why should this time be any different?"

That was when Mr. Govert, the greengrocer, pushed his way to the front of the crowd. "I'm not interested in who *started* this," he said. "What I want to know is who's going to pay for my fruit and vegetables."

"And my tables," the owner of the café added.

"And everything in front of *my* shop," said the man who sold postcards and buckets and spades.

Mr. Mesman held up his hand. "I will," he said.

The three shopkeepers looked surprised.

"I'll pay for everything that was damaged," Mr. Mesman said. "Islander or visitor, I'll pay for every scrap of damage, right down to the last guilder. And I'd like to offer everybody here right now a free drink, inside, at my expense. It's the least I can do to compensate you for all the distress you've had to suffer."

As he spoke, Flip saw Uncle Andries's shoulders slump. All of a sudden he looked like an old, old man who could hardly stand up on his own. When the crowd began to disperse, filing into the hotel, Flip found out why.

"Of course," Mr. Mesman continued, stepping close to Uncle Andries, "I *will* be wanting all that money back. Not just for the shops, but for what your horse did to my terrace. And it *is* your horse, living on your property, so that makes you liable for everything. I'll be wanting *you* to repay me."

"But he can't!" Flip protested. "He doesn't have enough money to pay for all the damage!"

Uncle Andries turned and looked down at Flip. "I know that," he said sadly. "And Mr. Mesman knows it too. Just like he also knows that I *do* have something I can sell to raise the money. Don't you, Mr. Mesman?"

Mr. Mesman smiled for real then. But it was a cruel smile. It reminded Flip of a cat about to pounce on a mouse.

"Yes," he said, "you do. But I'll offer you a good price for your farm. A very good price. In fact, once you've paid me back for all the damage, you'll still have a nice tidy sum left over. I don't want to leave you with *nothing*, you know."

Still smiling, he turned and walked away.

Uncle Andries went down the steps to the street. Flip followed him, guiding Storm.

"It really *wasn't* Storm's fault—" Flip began.

Uncle Andries cut him off. "I wish I'd never seen this blasted horse in my life!" he barked. He was angrier than Flip had ever seen him. "He's been nothing but trouble from the moment he arrived. He's put your life in danger. He's put Renske's life in danger. He won't do a lick of work for the farm. And now he's *cost* us the farm! Now we've lost everything my family's worked for almost one hundred years! I wish he'd never set *foot* on Moss—"

He stopped in mid-sentence as the horse drew level with him. Up close, he could now see the bloody welts the Mesman Boys' stones had raised on Storm's neck and flanks. All at once his expression softened and he rested his hand gently on the animal's neck. This time, Storm didn't shy away from his touch.

"Oh, you poor creature," he whispered. "No wonder you ran. No wonder." Then he turned to Flip. "You were right," he said. "You were telling the truth and I didn't believe you. I was too angry to stop and think. I owe you an apology."

Flip didn't know what to say. He'd never seen his uncle look so confused. Or heard him talk like this.

"Come along," Uncle Andries continued quietly. "Let's get him home and see to those wounds."

The three of them set off. When they reached the front of the hotel, they saw Mr. Mesman and his sons standing outside. The brothers were still carrying their slingshots.

Uncle Andries stopped. "Please wait a moment, Flip," he said.

He strode up to the boys and in one swift, fluid movement snatched the slingshots from their fingers. Then he ripped them to pieces with his bare hands. The veins on his neck stood out and his face went red with the effort, but when he was finished, there was nothing left but scraps of wood and strips of shredded rubber. He flung the fragments on the ground and stared the hotel owner straight in the eye.

"You can add the cost of those to the bill too!" he said, before following Flip and Storm back to the farm in silence.

Flip returned to the village later that afternoon, after he'd cleaned Storm's wounds and put him inside the barn, with Leila in the next stall for company. He was looking for his mom's letter. But though he walked up and down the street several times and even got down on his hands and knees to crawl under the hotel terrace, he didn't find a sign of it anywhere.

The one last thing connecting him to his mother and his old life in Amsterdam had vanished.

Completely.

32 * More Bad News

THE DAY AFTER Storm's rampage, Uncle Andries put on his suit, Aunt Elly put on her best overcoat, and the two of them walked into the village. They didn't say where they were going when they left, and they didn't say where they'd been when they returned. But they both looked sad and disappointed. The following day, the two of them got dressed up again and left the farm right after breakfast.

"They're going to the mainland," Mr. Bouten explained when Flip asked what was happening.

"Why?"

"They've got an appointment with the bank. They're going to see if they can borrow enough money to pay back Mesman." The old man shook his head. "But they won't be able to."

"Why not?"

"Farms like your uncle's are too expensive nowadays. Just getting to and from the island on the ferry's an expense the mainland farms don't have. I don't think there's a bank in the country would want to invest in this place. They'd all be worried they wouldn't earn their money back."

"But there has to be *something* someone can do," Flip said. "This farm can't go just because of Storm. That's not fair!"

"No," Mr. Bouten said, "it's not. But that Mesman's a clever one. He saw what Storm did and he knew right then and there how to use it to get what he always wanted. He knew your uncle couldn't pay for the damages, so he jumped in quick and paid them all."

"But why won't the *shopkeepers* let Uncle Andries pay them back?"

"They would," Mr. Bouten said. "The people who own the shops and the café would be happy to. That's what they said yesterday, when your aunt and uncle went into the village. They were happy to change their minds. It was that Mesman what wouldn't. Now he's got a chance to get his hands on this farm, he's not going to throw it away."

"But where are we going to go? What's going to happen to us?" Flip asked. "And what about Storm?"

Mr. Bouten shook his head. "I don't know, Flip. I honestly don't."

Flip left him standing in the yard and walked down to the field. Storm's wounds were healing fast and the two horses were back outside. As Flip climbed up onto the gate, Storm came trotting over to see if there was anything to eat. But he soon seemed to sense Flip's sadness and stopped looking. He stood still beside the gate, looking out over it and down the road.

A little later, Renske came out to join them. She climbed up beside Flip and stroked Storm's mane. There was no sign of the Ghost Girl. Since Storm's rampage through the village, she hadn't been seen at all. Flip wondered if she felt guilty for not backing up his story of what the Mesman Boys had done.

After a little while, Flip asked Renske if she'd like to ride Storm. She said yes and Storm let her. He walked slowly around the field with the little girl on his back, not at all his usual cheeky self. Then he let Flip ride him and that was how they passed the day, taking turns to walk around the field. Flip even managed a trot. Keeping his balance was hard and he fell off the first few times, but when he did, Storm always waited for him to climb back up and try again. By the end of the afternoon, he was riding around the field as though he'd been doing it all his life. It was so much fun he wished he could do it forever.

The two children were still outside when Aunt Elly and Uncle Andries trudged up the road toward them, late in the afternoon. They looked more tired and sad than they had the day before. Aunt Elly held out her hand to Renske.

"Come inside, my dear," she said. "I've got something to tell you."

"Just me?" Renske asked. "What about Flip?"

"Your father's going to talk to him," Aunt Elly said. "Now come inside."

Renske climbed down off the gate and followed her mother back to the farm. Flip jumped down beside his uncle.

"Did the bank say no?" he asked. "Mr. Bouten told me where you went."

For a moment, Uncle Andries looked puzzled, as though he had no idea what Flip was talking about. Then he shook his head and said, "No. I mean, yes, we went to the bank. And they did say no, which is what we expected. But that's not what I have to tell you, Flip. After we went to the bank, we went to see the police, to ask if they had any news about your mother. We thought since we were there, we might as well drop in. Save them a telephone call or a letter."

He hesitated. And right then and there, Flip knew what he was about to hear.

"Is she dead?" he asked quietly.

Uncle Andries looked down at him and nodded. "Yes," he said. "She is. It happened almost three years ago. In Germany. There was a fire in the hotel where she was working. Nobody knew who she was because she hadn't told them her real name and everything she had with her was destroyed in the flames. It was only when the police started looking for her after your *father* died that somebody finally put two and two together and identified her."

He paused for a few seconds.

"I am sorry, Flip," he said. "I really am very sorry."

Flip didn't say anything. He didn't know *what* to say. All this time he'd been waiting for his mom to come and take him away, only to discover that she couldn't have done so because she wasn't alive to do it. He'd been dreaming of something that could never, ever have happened. She was gone and he'd never see her again.

But there was other bad news too, he thought, as he looked up at Uncle Andries. Where would he and Aunt Elly and Renske live if they had to leave the farm? What would happen to them? What would happen to him?

And what would happen to Storm?

33 * Visitors

THE FARM WAS a quiet place in the days that followed. Uncle Andries milked the cows each morning and went out to work in the fields, but with every step he took he looked like a man carrying an enormous weight on his back. Aunt Elly cooked and cleaned and took the two children out into the vegetable garden to look after the plants. But after a few minutes she would usually slip away and Flip would find her sitting on an upturned wooden crate by the back door, gazing into space.

Neither of them minded at all when he asked if he could stay with Storm in the afternoons.

He no longer walked him, though. He fitted a halter to him in the field, led him down to the beach, climbed up onto his back, and trotted away along the sand.

Out under the early autumn sky, Flip felt all his worries fade away. As he splashed through the surf and then wound his way up through the dunes to the lighthouse, he forgot about everything and just let himself be carried away on a feeling of freedom he'd never known before in his life. It didn't last long, but while it did, he couldn't imagine a better place to be, or anything better to do.

Sometimes, Renske came with him. She liked being out with Storm too. But still there was no sign of the Ghost Girl. She'd become even more of a ghost. Aunt Elly said she'd heard in the village that Mrs. Elberg was planning to leave the island soon and go home. Flip rode past the cottage a few times but never saw either of them. He wondered if they'd leave without saying good-bye. It made him sad to think that one of the few friends he'd made on Mossum might leave without coming to see him at least one last time.

Then it was back to the farm, to the sad, silent kitchen and his sad and silent aunt and uncle, to wait to see what would happen next. To wait for Mr. Mesman to come and ask for his money. To wait for the farm to be sold.

The hotel owner appeared one week later. Flip was putting Storm back into the field and rubbing him down with an old towel. Uncle Andries was leaning on the gate. The two of them turned as Mr. Mesman strolled up the road, cigar in his mouth and hands in his pockets.

"Good afternoon," Uncle Andries said.

Mr. Mesman didn't take the cigar out of his mouth or his hands out of his pockets. "I thought you should know," he said, "that I've got some investors coming to the island. They'll be going over my plans for the new hotel and looking at the property, so if you see a group of strangers walking about, that'll be them. They've said if they're happy with things, I can expect a deal within the week."

"I see," Uncle Andries said.

"If we *do* agree to a deal," Mr. Mesman continued, "that's when I'll expect *you* to sign over the farm to me. I want to be clear. I wouldn't want there to be any misunderstandings between us."

This time, Uncle Andries didn't say anything. He just nodded.

"Excellent!" said Mr. Mesman, and strolled off back to his hotel. His cigar was still in his mouth and his hands were still in his pockets.

Uncle Andries walked back to the farm with Flip. "That's interesting," he said.

"What is?" Flip asked.

"He said he'll expect me to sell if the *investors* agree to a deal. It's as if he's waiting for them to give him some money. As if he needs *them* to pay *him* before *he* can pay *me*."

Flip felt a sudden wave of excitement race through him. "You mean if they don't agree, then Mesman won't have any money and we won't have to leave?"

"Possibly, Flip. Possibly. And it's *Mr.* Mesman. No need to be forgetting our manners."

Then Uncle Andries fell silent, lost in his own private thoughts.

The investors arrived the day after, on the midday ferry. There were four of them. They were all big round men wearing suits and ties and polished shoes, and they all smoked even bigger cigars than Mr. Mesman. At teatime, they gathered at the edge of Uncle Andries's farm. Mr. Mesman pulled maps and sketches of his proposed hotel from a big leather briefcase. Flip saw two of the visitors nodding their heads. The other two didn't look quite so convinced.

Great, Flip thought. *If two of them don't like it, there may not be any money. The sale might not go through!*

The five men set off toward the beach. When they returned, Flip was still out in the field. This time, all four visitors were nodding their heads vigorously, looking pleased. And Flip heard what Mr. Mesman said as he led them back down the road.

"Just wait until tomorrow," he said, beaming. "Wait until you've been out on the boat and seen the *whole* island. Then I think you'll see you've made the right decision."

Flip's heart sank. *The right decision* sounded as though the visitors *had* decided to invest in the new hotel. And if they'd done that, then there was no hope at all.

The farm really would be sold.

34 * A Warning Ignored

THE NEXT MORNING, when Mr. Bouten arrived at the farm, he brought more news about Mr. Mesman's boat trip around the island. It would start at midday and there would be a picnic lunch on board. The hotel owner had had the best food and drink brought in especially from the mainland. He was going to steer the boat himself.

"Won't do him any good, though," said Mr. Bouten. "Storm coming."

Flip looked out of the window. The sun was shining. There wasn't a cloud in the sky, or a trace of a breeze.

Mr. Bouten saw him looking. "Oh, it's coming," he said. "Be here midday. Or thereabouts."

"That's when you say the boat's going out," Aunt Elly said.

Mr. Bouten nodded.

Uncle Andries pushed his chair back from the table and stood up. "Then we have to warn them," he said.

"Didn't think you'd be worried about what happened to *him*," Mr. Bouten said. "Solve all your problems, that would. A nice rough sea for his visitors wouldn't make them so keen to invest."

"It probably wouldn't," Uncle Andries said. "But I can't let him go out in a storm. Whatever I think of him."

"Well, he won't listen," Mr. Bouten said. "Certainly not to you."

"We still have to warn him," Uncle Andries insisted. "We're lifeboat men. It's our duty."

Mr. Bouten looked up at him for a second. "You're right," he said. "We are. And I'll come with you to do it." But as he stood he added, "He won't listen, though. I guarantee you that."

And he was right. Mr. Mesman didn't.

Flip went with them to the hotel. When they stepped inside, he saw the four visitors in the lounge, laughing and smiling over cups of coffee. Mr. Mesman spotted Uncle Andries and hurried across to him.

"Well, well," he said with a smile. "Have you come to sign? Bit early for—"

"I've come to warn you," Uncle Andries said.

Mr. Mesman's smile vanished. "Warn me? About what?"

"About the storm coming."

Mr. Mesman frowned, then went to the front door and stepped out into the street. He looked up at the sky in all directions. The sun shone down. There was still no wind.

"A storm?" he said, looking as though it were the silliest thing he'd ever heard in his life. "Who told you that?"

"Me," said Mr. Bouten.

"Really?" Mr. Mesman's mocking look had only increased.

"He used to be a fisherman," Uncle Andries said. Flip could hear the barely contained anger in his voice. "He's forgotten more about bad weather than you could learn in a dozen lifetimes. If he says a storm's coming, it is."

"You know what I think," Mr. Mesman said, putting his hands in his pockets and smiling a smile that was anything but friendly. "*I* think you're just trying to put a stop to my little trip. *I* think you're trying to make me look bad in front of the investors."

"For heaven's sake!" Uncle Andries shouted. "I'm trying to *warn* you!"

"And I don't believe you," Mr. Mesman replied. He turned around and went in to join the investors.

Mr. Bouten turned to Uncle Andries. "Well," he said, "he didn't listen. What do you want to do now?"

"There's only one thing we *can* do," Uncle Andries said. "Get the lifeboat ready. Then we can rescue the idiot the moment he gets into trouble."

The three of them set off for the farm. They'd just reached the entrance when they were stopped by Mrs. Elberg. Her shoes were muddy and her hair was in disarray. Her eyes were red with fatigue.

"Have you seen Sophie?" she asked. "We're supposed to be leaving this afternoon but she got terribly upset when I started packing, and ran off. And now I can't find her anywhere. I've been all the way down to The Yellow and back and nothing. Not a trace."

The two men shook their heads. Mrs. Elberg turned hopefully to Flip, but he had to say he hadn't seen her either.

"She doesn't want to be out in what's coming," Mr. Bouten said. He told her about the approaching storm.

"Can you help me find her?" Mrs. Elberg sounded almost desperate now.

Looking uncomfortable, Uncle Andries shook his head and explained about Mr. Mesman's boat trip. "We have to get to the lifeboat. There'll be five lives at risk. We can't ignore them."

"No, of course not," Mrs. Elberg said. "I couldn't ask you to do that."

"*I'll* look for her," Flip said.

Uncle Andries shook his head. "I want you safe at home."

"Mr. Bouten just said she shouldn't be outside in what's coming!" Flip protested.

"She shouldn't. And neither should you."

But Flip wouldn't budge. "You're going to go out in the lifeboat," he said. "To rescue someone. Let me do the same. Let me rescue *Sophie*."

"You don't even know where to look."

Flip pointed to the east. "You haven't been that way, have you?" he asked Mrs. Elberg.

"No," she said. "Not yet."

"Then that's where I'll go. If I take Storm, I can go even faster. And Mr. Bouten said the storm won't be here till midday. That gives me a couple of hours."

"No!" Uncle Andries said.

"Why?" Flip demanded.

"Because you're only twelve!"

Mr. Bouten interrupted. "Andries, there were grown men up on that hotel terrace the day Storm ran off. I didn't see a single one of them who got him under control. But Flip here did. He was the only one brave enough to pull it off. And he didn't hesitate for a second to do it."

Uncle Andries stood still, lost in thought. After a while he looked down at Flip as though he'd never looked at him properly before.

"Can you *really* get her back on your own? And I do mean on your own. I don't want Renske going with you, no matter what she says. She's too little."

"Yes," Flip said, staring straight back at his uncle. "If she's out there, I can find her. And I can bring her back safely."

"Oh, Flip, if you could," Mrs. Elberg said. "She might listen to you! You might be the only person she *would* listen to."

"Right, then," Uncle Andries said to his nephew. "Fetch what you need."

Flip ran to the barn, grabbed a halter and a rope, and ran back. Uncle Andries was still waiting for him. The farmer hesitated, then reached out and patted his nephew's shoulder.

"You're a good lad, Flip," he said. "You've turned out well. I didn't think you would but you have. And I'm proud of you."

"We *all* are," Mr. Bouten added.

"Yes," Uncle Andries agreed. "We all are. Now go and find Sophie and get her back home." And with that, he turned and strode off toward the lifeboat station with Mr. Bouten at his side.

Flip ran to the field, fitted the halter, and climbed up onto Storm's back. Soon he was trotting along the path, past an anxious-looking Mrs. Elberg, and then overtaking Uncle Andries and Mr. Bouten.

When they were no more than specks in the distance, he wheeled Storm left and made his way down through the woods and the dunes. The faintest of breezes ruffled his hair as he rode out onto the beach. On the horizon, a smudge of darkness broke the clear blue of the sky.

Just as Mr. Bouten had predicted, the storm was coming.

35 * *Alarm*

TO THE WEST, there was nothing to see but empty sand stretching away to the horizon. In front of Flip, a family of vacationers was building a sand castle. To his right—east—far away in the distance, he saw shapes ambling along at the water's edge. Trotting up to them through the surf, he discovered it was just another group of vacationers. When he described the Ghost Girl, though, and asked if they'd seen her, he was told they had. Up near the lighthouse.

Urging Storm forward, Flip galloped up the path to the lighthouse. But she wasn't there. He stopped and gazed down along the island.

Before him lay the village and the church tower, the fields and the farms and the long golden sprawl of The Yellow. Out to sea on his left was the ferry coming in from the mainland, sunlight sparkling off its windows as it headed into the harbor. And there, at the end of a second smaller jetty, lay the little boat Mr. Mesman had hired for his trip. Flip could see him bustling about on board and the four investors taking their places in the seats at the stern. The sky on the southern side of the island was still so clear that Flip could see the sun shining on a white linen tablecloth, and on the bottles and glasses stacked on top of it.

To his right, far out in the North Sea, the smudge of darkness had grown into three thin fingers of cloud poking up over the horizon. As he watched, they grew longer and wider. Another gust of wind pushed the hair off his forehead.

He looked back down to the harbor, where he saw Mr. Mesman's boat cast off and chug happily away from the jetty. And then into view directly below him, wandering along the beach at the base of the dunes, came the Ghost Girl.

He backed away so she wouldn't look up and see them. How was he going to get to her? He was pretty certain she'd run away from her mother because she didn't want to leave Mossum. What if she thought Flip was part of a group of people who had come to find her and she ran away again? Then he had an idea. What if she only saw Storm?

Slipping off the horse's back, he waited until the Ghost Girl had disappeared behind a dune, then descended as quickly and quietly as he could toward the beach. As soon as he reached a fork in the path, he let go of Storm and urged him forward, to the left. Flip ran around to the right. His plan worked perfectly.

Storm strolled out onto the beach, almost directly in front of the Ghost Girl. The moment she saw him she stopped. Instantly, Storm stopped too. She looked around to see if anyone was with him and, seeing no one, walked slowly toward him with her hand held out.

Behind Flip, the wind was picking up. The thin fingers of cloud on the horizon had now grown into big grasping claws trailing black strands of rain. When he emerged from the dunes, sand was blowing off the tops and against his back. He couldn't believe how fast the weather was changing. It definitely helped him, though, because neither Storm nor the Ghost Girl had heard him approaching.

She saw him and tried to run, but Flip caught her arm and held tight.

"Your mom's looking for you," he said.

She heaved and pulled but it was no good. She couldn't break Flip's grip.

"Come on," he said. "Get up beside me and we'll ride back home."

She shook her head.

The wind whipped at their hair and clothes. Above them, the blue sky was vanishing behind a rolling wave of cloud. The temperature was dropping fast. Drops of rain began to splatter down on the sand around them.

"You don't want to get caught in this," he said.

She shook her head again.

"Look," he said, "I'm not angry with you."

From the way her eyes widened, he knew what she was thinking, even if she wouldn't say it. *Really?*

"The only ones I'm angry with are the Mesman Boys and their dad. Not you."

Another *really?*

"Yes," he said. And then he knew just what to say. "So can we go home, please, before Storm gets completely soaked?"

It was exactly the right thing to say. She stopped struggling and looked at the horse. Her face softened and she nodded. Using a clump of sand and grass to stand on, Flip helped her up onto Storm's back, then climbed up behind her and set off along the beach.

As they rounded the eastern tip of the island, the lifeboat siren began to wail.

36 * *Lightning Strike*

AT THE SOUND of the alarm, Flip reached around the Ghost Girl, wound his hands in Storm's mane, and urged him into a trot. When they swung around onto the northern shore, lightning flashed across the sky.

Flip saw the lifeboat in the distance, rolling across the sand to stop before a dark and muddy sea flecked with white foam breakers. He saw Mr. Bouten jump down from his cart and stride into the waves to find the right spot for a launch. It wasn't long before the horses had been unfastened and reattached to the rear of the trailer. Uncle Andries and the rest of the crew were pulling on their heavy-weather gear and climbing up into the lifeboat.

Another flash of lightning, closer this time, followed by a loud clap of thunder.

Storm didn't like the weather. His ears were pinned back flat on his head and his tail was flicking nervously from side to side. He stomped at the sand and snorted. He'd slowed to a walk by then and kept swinging to his left and his right. It took all Flip's strength to keep him going in a straight line. He didn't blame him for this behavior: the wind and the waves must have been bringing back lots of bad memories.

Beyond the dunes, in the woods, the tops of the trees were whipping back and forth. Flip could see the flagpole on the church tower actually bending. All that was left of the flag were a few tattered scraps of cloth snapping furiously in the wind.

Ahead of them, the horses were hauling the trailer into the waves. In a crash of spray, the lifeboat slid loose from its restraints and hit the water. It rolled back and forth as it righted itself, then the engine roared into life and it fought its way through the breakers and out to sea.

Lightning struck a third time, a dazzling fork of silver light so bright it was as though somebody had turned on a massive flashlight. For a moment the beach was illuminated like the inside of a room and Flip could see every single detail—the horses, the ropes, the men in green waders, and the sand-caked tracks on the trailer.

Then he heard a crash.

And it came from the village.

The fork of lightning that had struck just seconds before had hit the tree that grew beside the church tower. As Flip and the Ghost Girl watched, the top half of the massive elm folded in on itself, like somebody closing his fingers into a fist. Clumps of small branches were ripped loose. Leaves were torn away into the rain.

The falling trunk struck the side of the tower, ripped open a giant hole, and smashed away half the roof. Bricks and mortar, broken tiles, and wooden beams cascaded to the ground in a cloud of dust that the wind whipped apart in seconds. The flagpole wavered, broke free, and plummeted out of sight into the churchyard.

On the beach, the men by the lifeboat stood transfixed. They obviously couldn't believe what they'd seen and didn't know what to do.

But Mr. Bouten did. Flip saw him wave them away, into the village. They hesitated, but he insisted. Flip could tell from his hand movements that he was telling them to help at the church, that *he'd* uncouple the horses and get them onto the beach.

So they stripped off their waders, grabbed their shoes, and ran back through the dunes. As they disappeared from sight, Mr. Bouten strode out to the horses waiting in the surf. Alarmed by the ferocity of the weather, they were bucking and jerking from side to side, anxious to be free, making such a commotion that he had to focus all his energy on them to make sure they didn't knock him down. That was why he didn't see what was approaching.

It was a huge wave, higher and thicker than all the others that had preceded it, and it came rolling in from far out to sea, gathering speed and height and weight as it advanced. It hit Mr. Bouten in the back and slammed him headfirst into the trailer, then drove him under the surface and into the surf.

A moment later he reappeared, sprawled on his back at the water's edge. A fresh wave submerged him. When it receded, he was still on his back. And still not moving.

There was nobody to see it and nobody to help. Everyone was in the village, gathered at the church tower. The only ones who knew what had happened—and who could do anything about it—were the two children on the horse.

Flip didn't hesitate. Yelling at the Ghost Girl to hold tight, he urged Storm forward, down the beach toward the fallen man and the eight stranded horses.

37 * Into the Waves

As if he sensed the urgency of the situation, Storm broke from a trot into a canter and then a flat-out gallop. It was like some vast machine uncoiling itself and rumbling into action. He didn't need to be prompted. He hurtled along the beach with his hooves flying and his mane snapping and flapping in the wind. His breath came from his nostrils in short, shuddering bursts. His strides grew longer and the sound of his hooves on the sand was like distant thunder. Down the beach he flew, with Flip and the Ghost Girl clinging to his back with every scrap of strength they could summon and the wind roaring in their ears.

The lifeboat trailer drew closer. Flip could see the horses in the water on both sides rearing their heads, neighing, and kicking futilely in their harnesses. Behind them, Mr. Bouten lay motionless in the surf.

Flip jumped from Storm's back, pulled the Ghost Girl down after him, and ran to the old man's side. He was unconscious and there was a gash in his forehead from where he'd been thrown against the trailer. Blood had soaked his face and his clothes.

The two of them tried pulling him up out of the water but they couldn't move him. He was too heavy. As Flip tried to think what to do, he heard a snort behind him and looked up into Storm's eyes.

Of course, he thought. He ran to the cart, found a length of rope, looped it under Mr. Bouten's arms, and tied it in a knot over his chest. The other end he tied around Storm's neck. Grabbing the halter, he urged him back up the beach.

In four easy strides, Storm pulled the old man out of the sea and onto dry land. Flip knelt beside Mr. Bouten and saw that he was still breathing. But before he could do anything else, terrified whinnies from the sea pulled him away.

All eight horses were bucking and kicking, trying to escape from the waves crashing in on them. There was no sign of anyone from the village. And worse, Flip realized, no time to go and get them.

Each horse had a thick canvas harness around its neck and shoulders, and each harness was attached to the trailer by two big ropes that ran down the horse's flanks to a wooden cross brace and then to the trailer. But Flip couldn't see how they were fixed to the trailer because it was now under the water. Fear flashed through him. What was he going to do? Where did he start?

Then he saw it. If he could cut the ropes between the horses and the cross brace, they'd be free. They'd still be wearing the harnesses but they'd be free. He dropped to his knees, hunted through Mr. Bouten's pockets, found his knife, and pulled it loose. As he opened the blade, the Ghost Girl jumped down from the cart with a length of thin rope. She grabbed the knife, fastened one end of the rope to the metal loop on the handle, and tied the other tight around Flip's wrist. He turned and ran into the surf.

The first wave hit him in the chest and knocked him down. He came up spitting out water and spluttering for air, wiping his hair from his eyes. Before the second wave could strike, he pushed himself forward and grabbed the edge of the trailer to hold himself steady. Then he reached out, grabbed the first rope, and started cutting.

The blade was sharp. It went through the rope in seconds. A moment later, the second parted. When the horse felt the pressure on its chest and shoulders loosen, it kicked forward. But it didn't break loose. Instantly, Flip saw why. Another rope, attached to its halter, bound it to the halter of the horse on its right. Flip had to free two horses before either one could escape.

He clawed his way back down to the second horse's rope and cut again. Finally freed, both animals stumbled forward, regained their balance, and turned and splashed up onto the beach. The Ghost Girl grabbed the ends of the trailing ropes and fastened them to Mr. Bouten's cart.

Flip didn't see this. He'd already moved on to the next pair. Again the knife did its work. Within minutes, the third and fourth horses were splashing up onto the beach to join their companions, and only too happy to be fastened to the cart by the Ghost Girl.

Soaked from head to foot, shaking and shivering, Flip now waded through chest-high water and around to the other side of the trailer. He hadn't been in the sea long but his fingers were cold and beginning to lose their feeling. If the knife hadn't been tied to his wrist, he would have dropped it long ago.

There was still no sign of anyone from the village.

He grabbed the first rope he came to and started cutting. As he did so, a massive wave crashed into the line of horses, swept around their heads, picked Flip up, and threw him onto the beach. He got up, shook his head, and staggered back into the water.

It was up past the animals' shoulders now, fast approaching their necks. All four were bucking and kicking and struggling desperately. But the ropes were strong and the canvas harnesses even stronger. Designed for hauling a lifeboat trailer, they wouldn't break if fifty horses tried to pull them apart.

Flip sawed and hacked, not even counting anymore, just concentrating on cutting. The fifth and sixth horses were freed and scrambled to safety. Now there were only two to go. But severing the ropes for the seventh horse took twice the time the sixth had. His arms were aching, and his fingers were turning numb. As he dragged himself forward to the eighth horse, a wave he didn't see coming slammed him against the trailer tread. He felt an icy flash of pain in his shoulder. Before he could lift his head, a second wave pushed him under, and a third drove him up onto the beach.

He lay on his side, almost too tired to breathe. As he watched, the heads of the last two horses vanished beneath the swell. It was only for an instant, and then they emerged again, eyes wide with fear, mouths open and gasping for air. He knew they were only minutes away from drowning.

He looked around for the Ghost Girl, to ask for her help. But he couldn't see her. There was no sign of her anywhere. With a sudden flash of anger, he realized she'd run off and left him yet again. If she had, that meant the only chance of survival the horses now had lay with him. Ignoring his trembling arms and legs, Flip pushed himself upright and staggered back into the waves.

He grabbed for a rope, only to be knocked sideways by a breaker. He swallowed seawater, coughed and spat it out. He struggled forward. Another wave pushed him back, but this time he felt something behind him, holding him steady, supporting him. He looked around into two big eyes and a breath of hot air from flaring nostrils. It was Storm. With the water surging and crashing around him, the horse was supporting Flip, keeping him in place.

It was all he needed. He reached out, wrapped his arm around the remaining ropes, and with the last of his strength, started cutting. The first rope parted. He moved to the second and began again. But his fingers were now so cold and numb he could hardly hold the knife—he kept dropping it. He just didn't have the strength to finish the job.

He didn't need to, though. All the time he'd been cutting, the terrified horse had been jerking and twisting its head. And it was the jerking and twisting that finally broke the partly severed rope in two. Freed at last, the final two horses swung around and struggled up onto dry land with water streaming from their flanks.

Flip turned and scrabbled for the rope attached to Storm's halter. Grabbing it with both hands, he managed to hang on just long enough for Storm to pull him to safety. When he let go, his head hit the sand with a thump that made his teeth rattle.

That was when he heard a noise, coming from far away. Glancing up, he saw a stream of villagers pouring out of the dunes. And right out in front of them, running for all she was worth, was the Ghost Girl.

38 ✳ *A New Home*

When Flip woke up, he was lying in a wooden box. There were planks above him, beside him, and down by his feet. But he was also warm and dry, wearing pajamas and tucked up beneath a big thick quilt.

That was when he realized where he was: in Renske's bed, in the kitchen, at the farm.

Sitting at the kitchen table, drinking cups of coffee and eating apple pie, were his aunt and his uncle, Renske, and Mr. Bouten. And beside them sat the Ghost Girl and Mrs. Elberg.

They didn't look like they usually looked and it took him a while to work out what it was about them that was different. When he realized, he laughed.

They were smiling.

Both of them.

Then the Ghost Girl looked over at him and he got another shock.

"You're awake," she said.

"You're *talking*!" he said.

"I've been talking for a *day* now!" she said.

There was a brightness in her eyes Flip had never seen before. Even though her face was still even paler than her hair, and her eyes were as round as ever, he didn't think she looked like the Ghost Girl anymore. She was lively. Excited. *Happy.* It was as if the Ghost Girl was gone, gone for good now, and in her place was . . . Sophie.

Then Flip frowned. "How long have I been asleep?"

"More than twenty-four hours!" Renske said, running to his side. "It's six o'clock. In the evening. Last night I slept in your bed. In the barn. And I wasn't scared *once*!"

Flip sat up. The grown-ups had left the table and gathered in front of him. He looked at Mr. Bouten, who had a bandage around his head and bruised and blackened eyes. But he was smiling too, and he leaned over and patted Flip's shoulder.

"I owe you a big thank-you," he said. "I heard what you did."

"*We* did," Flip said. "Storm and me. *He* pulled you out of the water."

Mr. Bouten nodded. "He did. But he wouldn't have done it if you hadn't taken him down to the sea in the first place. He's a clever horse, but he's not *that* clever."

"Is he all right?" Flip asked.

"He's fine," Uncle Andries said. "He's out in the field with Leila."

"What he's doing?"

"Eating," said Renske. "And rolling. We cleaned him up but he went straight out and had a roll."

"Can I see him?" Flip asked, and started to get out of bed.

"Soon," Aunt Elly said, pushing him back. "You just lie still for a while."

Flip looked at Uncle Andries. "What happened to the boat?" he asked. "Did you rescue them?"

"We rescued *everyone*," Uncle Andries said. "We got them all off safely and brought them back. And just in time. The engine had broken down and they were drifting out to sea. The waves out there would have swamped them in minutes. That boat wasn't built for the North Sea in a thunderstorm."

There was a moment's silence. Flip looked at Mrs. Elberg. "Are you leaving now?" he asked. "Going back to The Hague?"

She looked different somehow, as if the sound of her daughter's voice had brought *her* life back too. "Oh," she said, finishing her coffee and putting her cup down, "we're not leaving. We've got a new house now, Sophie and me."

"Where?"

"Here," Mrs. Elberg said. "On Mossum."

"We're going to live in the hotel," Sophie blurted out. "Mama bought it."

"You *bought* it?" Flip said. "But that means there'll be two hotels when Mr. Mesman builds his new one."

Mrs. Elberg shook her head. "He's not going to build a new hotel. All *he's* going to do is leave the island and take his three boys with him."

"And *not come back*!" Renske said.

"Why?" Flip asked. "What happened?"

"Well, for a start," Mrs. Elberg said, "when the investors found out he'd ignored the storm warning from your uncle and Mr. Bouten, they were furious. They didn't feel like going into business with a man who'd almost gotten them drowned. So they left. But," she went on, "I spoke to one of them before they did, and he told me Mr. Mesman doesn't have any money. He did some checking up before he came and found out that Mr. Mesman doesn't even have enough to buy your uncle's farm. He certainly hasn't got enough for a new hotel. That's why he needed investors. And Mr. Mesman realized that once the story about the boat and the storm got out, he'd find it very difficult to attract any other investors. So when I offered to buy the hotel, he said yes."

"Are you rich?" Flip asked.

Mrs. Elberg smiled, a real smile with no sadness in it at all. "I'm rich enough to buy a hotel from a man who doesn't have much money," she said. "And can't argue about the price."

"*And* she paid for the damage Storm did," Renske said. "So *we* don't have to leave the island either."

Flip was confused. "But I thought you didn't like it here. I thought Mossum was a disappointment. Because it hadn't helped Sophie." It felt strange saying her real name. But, he thought, it sounded much better than the Ghost Girl.

Mrs. Elberg shook her head. "I've spent the last nine months going back and forth from here to there and every doctor in between, trying to find someone who could help Sophie speak. *None* of them worked. And neither did Mossum. But then she met *you*."

Flip wasn't sure he'd heard right. "*Me?*" he said.

"If it hadn't have been for you, she wouldn't have run up the beach to get help when you were saving the horses. That's where she went and that's when she spoke. She had to, to get people to understand. To get them to come and help."

"And once I started," Sophie broke in, "it got easier and easier and I could say lots of other words."

"So I asked myself," Mrs. Elberg continued, "why I would leave the one place where something *good* had finally happened to my daughter? Where she started speaking again? Not to mention smiling and laughing. And that's when I decided to stay. Now," she said, standing up and putting on her jacket, "I've got a thousand things to do, so we must be off. I hope, Flip, that when you're fully recovered you'll come and see us. And when you do, bring Storm with you. I might have a job for him."

"A job?"

"I'm thinking of having a horse-drawn carriage to bring guests up from the harbor. Storm's a handsome fellow, and now you've calmed him down and made him listen to others, I think he might enjoy pulling a carriage all by himself. It would give him a chance to show off, which I think is what he likes doing most of all." She walked to the door with her daughter. Just before she left, she turned back to Flip and pointed at the table. "There's a present for you, by the way. I thought you'd appreciate it."

When the two of them had left, Aunt Elly helped Flip out of the bed and sat him down at the kitchen table in front of a parcel wrapped in thick brown paper.

He opened it . . . to find his record player!

"Mrs. Elberg thought you'd like it back," Uncle Andries said. "So now you can play those records you brought with you."

"Down here?" Flip asked.

"No," Uncle Andries said. "In your room."

"But there's no elec—" Flip began.

Uncle Andries held up his hand. "Did you know Mr. Bouten was an electrician?"

Flip shook his head.

"One of his many talents," Uncle Andries said. "And as soon as he's better, he's running a cable up to your room. You'll have a proper light. And you'll be able to play your records."

Flip hardly knew what to say. He couldn't take in all the changes and developments. But despite the good news, there was really only one thing he was interested in.

"May I go and see Storm?" he asked. "Just for a few minutes?"

Uncle Andries looked at Aunt Elly.

"Do you feel dizzy?" she asked.

Flip shook his head.

"Can you stand up, close your eyes, and touch your nose with your forefinger without looking?"

Flip did it with *both* forefingers.

"Are you hungry?"

"I'm starving!"

Aunt Elly smiled and nodded. "Then you can get dressed and see Storm while I make you something to eat. Then it's straight back to bed with you."

Flip nodded and, before anyone could change their minds, threw on some clothes, grabbed a carrot from the larder, and dashed out into the yard and across to the field.

Storm was all the way at the far end of the field when he heard Flip climb onto the gate. His ears pricked up, he let out a long loud whinny, and he turned and galloped toward him.

Flip hid the carrot in his pocket. Storm found it and gobbled it down in seconds. When he was finished, he let out a soft snort of contentment and lowered his head.

"I know," Flip said, resting his forehead against Storm's muzzle and stroking his neck. "I missed you too."

And that was how the two of them stayed while the sun sank in the sky, while the shadows stretched out across the farm, and while darkness settled slowly, ever so slowly, on the island.

On Flip and Storm's new home.

Acknowledgments

Three people helped enormously with the writing of *Storm Horse* and I would like to thank them here: my agent, Catherine Pellegrino; Chicken House editor Imogen Cooper; and my sister, Patricia Waldron. It wouldn't have become what it is without you.

About the Author

Nick Garlick was born in 1954 and lived, worked, or went to school in just about every part of England before moving to the Netherlands in 1990.

His first book, *California Dreaming*, was a science fiction thriller published in 1981. After many years working as a freelance technical writer, copywriter, editor, and translator, he published his first two children's stories with Andersen Press.

He now lives with his wife and a vegetable-eating cat in the city of Utrecht, where he's currently working on more children's stories.